BETWEEN THE DEVIL & THE DEEP BLUE SEA

A KENT BROTHERS NOVELLA

ELIZABETH ESSEX

All rights reserved.

No part of this publication may be sold, copied, distributed, reproduced or transmitted in any form or by any means, mechanical or digital, including photocopying and recording or by any information storage and retrieval system without the prior written permission of both the publisher, Oliver Heber Books and the author, Elizabeth Essex, except in the case of brief quotations embodied in critical articles and reviews.

PUBLISHER'S NOTE: This is a work of fiction. Names, characters, places, and incidents either are the product of the author's imagination or are used fictitiously. Any resemblance to actual persons, living or dead, business establishments, events, or locales is entirely coincidental.

Copyright © 2016 by Elizabeth Essex

THE DEVIL's OWN LUCK

Copyright © 2021 by Elizabeth Essex

Original Copyright as *"A MERRY DEVIL"*

© 2017 by Elizabeth Essex

Excerpt from ALMOST A SCANDAL

Copyright © 2019 by Elizabeth Essex

for revised edition; original copyright 2012.

All rights reserved.

All rights reserved.

Published by Oliver-Heber Books

Edited by Erica Monroe at Quillfire Author Services

Cover Design by Forever After Romance Designs

Photography by Killian Group & Shutterstock

0 9 8 7 6 5 4 3 2 1

PRAISE FOR ELIZABETH ESSEX

ALMOST A SCANDAL

"*Almost a Scandal* is a bold and brazen fast paced romance with a daring heroine and smoldering hot hero! With an explosive danger and red-hot romance this book is most definitely a book to treasure!" ~ *Publisher's Weekly*

"Essex will have readers longing to set sail alongside her daring heroine and dashing hero. This wild ride of a high seas adventure/desire-in-disguise romance has it all: nonstop action, witty repartee and deft plotting.

From the bow to the mast, from battles to ballrooms, Essex delivers another reckless bride and another read to remember." ~ *Romantic Times*

"The first book in the Reckless Brides Trilogy is a seafarer's delight. Col and Sally's high stakes adventure is fast-paced and fraught with peril. Well-timed humor punctuates the action and the use of frigate-speak adds authenticity to the shipboard dialog.

The love story teases the reader at first, as Col and Sally struggle to conceal their attraction on board the Audacious. Then things turn desperate when the circumstances of war seem intent on driving them apart. A smartly written, emotional tempest." ~ *Reader to Reader Reviews*

A BREATH OF SCANDAL

"Essex's second Reckless Bride certainly suits the title. The bold heroine easily wins readers' hearts, along with her officer and gentleman hero. Essex brings a breath of fresh and funny air to the Regency while her stylish writing and intelligent characters appeal to hearts and minds. Pure, delicious, sexy pleasure awaits readers." ~ *Romantic Times Book Reviews*

"Creating two very strong-willed characters and a mouthwatering romance, Ms. Essex has penned a deliciously compelling and heartwarming story that will keep the reader glued to the pages until the very end." ~ *Affaire de Coeur Magazine*

AFTER THE SCANDAL

"The inner growth of [the characters] coupled with the fast-paced action of the murder mystery makes this one intense, interesting adventure romance. [O]verall this is one smooth ride of a novel. Most of all, I am delighted by the turnout of this murder mystery. Elizabeth Essex has crafted a thoroughly interesting novel full of mystery, intrigue, and fascinating characters. I mean, who ever heard of a *thieving* duke?" ~ *Buried Under Romance*

"An exciting romantic tale that is guaranteed to weave a spell around you!! FANTASTICALLY WELL DONE!!!" ~ *Addicted to Romance*

A SCANDAL TO REMEMBER

"Set sail with Essex as she cleverly pits a bluestocking against a stiff-upper-lipped British naval officer and lets the sparks fly. Essex spices her fast-paced tale with fascinating details of ships and sailing and adds plenty of sexual tension, high-seas adventures, danger and desire. Readers will be on the edges of their seats reading this latest Reckless Brides tale." ~ *Romantic Times*, 4 ½ stars and TOP PICK!

"Essex's fifth Reckless Brides novel takes readers on another harrowing high seas adventure, filled from jib to mizzen with deception, sabotage, peril and surprise." ~ *Reader to Reader Reviews*

MAD FOR LOVE

"It's a fast-paced quick read that simply sparkles; the writing is deft and humorous." ~ *All About Romance*

MAD ABOUT THE MARQUESS

"This book is delightful…The dialogue is wonderful and sass wars are just about my favorite thing ever. The plot is just enough crazysauce layered on top of historical goodness. There was literally nothing about *Mad About the Marquess* that I didn't like." ~ *Smart B*tches, Trashy Books, A Review*

DEDICATION

For Erica Monroe,
fellow author and history enthusiast:
for your particularly welcome blend of sharp-eyed critique and
boundless enthusiasm,
and for always, always having my back,
I thank you from the bottom of my acerbic, bourbon-filled heart.

CHAPTER 1

*C*APTAIN HARRY BECK made his deliberate way up the steep, narrow street of Bocka Morrow in a vain attempt to escape the chilly, cheerless confines of his rooms at Castle Keyvnor and the endless childish bickering of his siblings. Harry was too weary for childishness—the omnipresent ache of his leg was a constant reminder that he'd left his childhood far behind.

He'd come out with the vague aim of reacquainting himself with the village where he had once spent a year under the tutelage of the Reverend Mr. Teague.

But no one spoke to him. Nary a soul.

He ought not to have worn his uniform, of course. Cornwall was a strange place, full of open secrets, covert alliances and unspoken agreements, and after twelve years, he was a stranger to them—a stranger in a navy uniform that made him not only conspicuous, but a damned object of derision.

He ought not have come to Cornwall at all. But his father the marquess had insisted upon his company. And when his father insisted, Harry—always the dutiful son—complied.

So here he was, in his weather-beaten blue sea coat, being shunned.

He turned at some slight sound to find two women in close conversation—a mother and daughter, he surmised—coming up the cobbles behind him. But no sooner had he raised his hat in polite greeting, than the older woman hauled to larboard up a side lane, towing the younger woman after her like a ship's boat on a loose painter.

But the younger woman—a girl as tall and lathy as a bowsprit—was looking at him over her shoulder with a strangely stunned look on her expressive face, a hint of a hopeful smile on her wide lips. As if he weren't a pariah. As if he were something altogether finer.

Nessa. Nessa Teague.

The name fell into his mind, rippling through his memory like a clear polished stone plunked into a well. Nessa Teague, the Reverend Schoolmaster Teague's daughter. The lass who had let him copy her Latin grammar and trigonometric projection exercises. The lass whose laugh had made him feel more at home in a stranger's household, whose rambles and explorations in the sailing dory in the bay had filled his days with sunshine and adventure. She had one of those distinctly Cornish faces—all wide, pixie-dashed blue eyes under dark, uncompromising brows. How could he ever have forgotten?

She raised her hand as if she would greet him. But she was already gone, towed around a corner and out of sight behind the barge of her mother, leaving Harry to make his way to the Crown & Anchor, a low public house along the quay, in a slightly more hopeful state of mind, if not of body.

Damn, but his leg ached something fierce.

It had been over six months since the cutting end of a French chain-shot had ripped through the mizzenmast of his frigate and wrecked its bloody way through his thigh. The resulting broken bone had been nigh unto healed when he'd taken a second peppering of canister shot in action a month ago, weakening the break, forcing him to be put ashore and sent home to Suffolk to convalesce. Within a day, Harry had thought he would go mad with inaction.

"Come with me to Cornwall," his father had suggested when Harry had clawed his stiff, painful way downwind to his father's library on his first morning home. "The trip will take your mind from your unpleasantness."

Unpleasantness. What a ridiculous euphemism for the injury that had damn near cost him his life, not to mention his leg. Or the years of service that had cost him his youth. Or any of the hardships he had endured in the name of family, King and country.

But his father was right—he did need some temporary occupation to take his mind off his injury. So, he had agreed to accompany his family, complete with his brothers—Anthony, the Viscount Redgrave and their father's heir, and Michael, the spare's spare—as well as his younger sister, Charlotte, to Castle Keyvnor where they had come to hear the will of Harry's late great uncle, the Earl of Banfield.

But Harry had no desire to be closeted away in the allegedly haunted and frankly gloomy castle where the Banfield will could have no interest or advantage to him—the dead earl not being known for leaving naval preferments or promotions to junior relations. And after twelve long years' absence at sea, during which he had received only intermittent letters from his family, and almost none from his brothers, Harry hardly knew them. They were all but strangers.

Which was why he found himself entering the shadowy confines of the public house well before noon. The place still held the dank salt stink of last night's spilled ale, but at least it wasn't crowded. A couple of drovers gulped down brown ale for elevenses, while a lone fisherman slouched in the corner—a fisherman who wasn't a fisherman at all.

He was Captain Matthew Kent of the Royal Navy, whom Harry had known for years, serving together as lieutenants in one ship or another. "Kent! What are you doing here?"

"God's balls," Kent griped under his breath as he hunched over a tankard. "Are you trying to get me killed? Don't come near me in that bloody uniform."

Instantly on his guard, Harry dropped his voice. "Surely you exaggerate. This is Cornwall, not Copenhagen."

"Gutted and left out to bleach like a bleeding pilchard," Kent avowed. "It's still a bloody battle, Becks." He took a long, seemingly disinterested draw from his tankard. "Heave to and stand off a bit, and tell me what in hell you're doing in this reeking place."

Harry moved off a pace or two and angled his shoulders as if he were watching the harbor out the window. "Family business."

Kent sent him a long look out of the corner of his eye. "Family business being the trade?"

The "trade" being a euphemism for smuggling—a highly profitable and entirely illegal endeavor that encompassed most of the coast and nearly all of the local residents. "No, an inheritance that may have some advantage for my father. But what of the trade? It's been going on here for years—a little brandy and a little lace, and everyone in the village lives a little better." Harry was too much of a pragmatist to let a little illegal activity get under his skin.

"Brandy and lace is one thing," Kent growled. "Secrets and munitions are entirely another."

Harry felt a cold fury slide under his skin and settle into his chest like an icy fog. Secrets and munitions *were* another thing entirely—secrets and munitions were treason. "Well, damn my eyes. From any other man, I might not believe it to be true."

Kent shrugged off the complimentary assessment of his character with a weary sort of skepticism. "The Admiralty have traced a long-standing leak in their bilge wash of information to this coast. I've been here nearly seven months and narrowed it to this particular village." He shied another sharp look around the room to make sure they were not being observed. "Where are you staying?"

"Castle Keyvnor." It was a dark, medieval hulk that loomed from the cliffs above the village like a glowering troll. After years spent in dank, dark ships, the castle held little of the terror that seemed to frighten some of the other, more susceptible guests, but still, Harry wouldn't mind an excuse to get out.

"I don't think there's any smuggling up there—their caves are old, but locked and empty," Kent mused. "How well do you know the village?"

"Not well. I spent some time here many years ago, taking tuition from the local vicar before I took my place as a midshipman." His father had chosen the Reverend Teague to tutor Harry—who had not been the best of schoolroom students—on the advice of his cousin the late Earl Banfield.

"You've been away too long."

"Too long for what?" Harry asked. "There must be a reason you're out of uniform and reeking like a haddock."

"Not now. Not here." Kent didn't meet his eye but kept his gaze resolutely out the window even as he spoke in a voice too low for the drovers to hear. "But I could use your help."

A fist of excitement landed a well-aimed blow to Harry's mid-beam. This was what he craved the way a sot wanted rum—purpose. "How?"

"There's a fête of sorts in a few days—the Feast of Saint Allan. Allantide they call it hereabouts."

Harry vaguely remembered the festival from his youth—a week of celebration in the name of a local saint that culminated in bonfires at All Hallows' Eve, followed by the far less pagan counterpoint of the Christian All Saints' Day. Such diversions had been one of the things he had missed most when he had been sent off to the harsher life at sea—a memory from what now seemed a carefree, golden youth. "Aye?"

"Come make merry and make yourself known, casual-like. Make free to buy a pint or two and invite folk to a bit of talk."

"Which folk?"

"Any and all—squires to squid rakers."

"And you?"

"I'll find you." Kent tipped up his tankard. "Casual-like. But for shite's sake, don't wear that damned blue coat."

Harry wanted to object—he rather liked the damned old salt-stained sea coat. He was uncomfortable not wearing it. It was his armor and shield—his very identity. Take him out of his uniform coat and he was just another invalid—worthless and without a profession.

But Kent was just like him—a navy man born and bred. And Matthew Kent wouldn't ask such a thing of him unless it were bloody-well important. "Aye," he finally agreed.

It was not the first time Harry and Kent had navigated the treacherous waters between the Devil and the deep blue sea. And it wasn't like to be the last.

Kent knocked back the last of his bitters and rose. "And Becks?"

"Aye?"

"You're a sight for damned sore eyes."

CHAPTER 2

BY THE SUNDAY before All Hallows' Eve, the village abounded with Allan apples, bright red and polished to a beckoning shine. The market and shops were brimming—even the Mermaid's Kiss Inn put a bowl out on the taproom counter.

But instead of buying an Allan apple—what little pocket money Nessa had for such an indulgence had always gone into the poor box—she decided to pick her own from the small orchard behind the manse. If magic existed, surely it lived in the unusual, the out-of-the-way and overlooked, and not in the shouty, shiny distractions of the everyday.

And so with a whispered prayer to Saint Allan to vouchsafe her first foray into heathenism, Nessa chose an unblemished Pendragon Red for its small size and good stem, important considerations for bobbing. She carved her mark—a tiny, feathered arrow shot through the Roman numeral II, "Nessa" being Cornish for second born—and secreted the apple deep in her pocket, polishing it surreptitiously throughout the day as she fetched and toted and did one chore after another in preparation for the village festival. And if her mother or father thought it odd that she should volunteer to take charge of the apple bobbing barrel instead of the cakes, they were too busy and too thankful for Nessa's usual thorough competence and gift for managing youngsters to question her motives.

"Good, harmless fun," her father judged. "Better for the younger set than the cross."

"The cross" was a game played by the more daring of the lads. Apples were suspended from a flat cross with lit candles on the top face, like a chandelier—the object being to bite an apple without tilting the cross and dripping hot wax onto one's face. Good harmless fun.

If one were a child. Which she probably was for hoping Captain Lord Harry Beck would remember the last time he had played such a game, and lost, and come to her for consolation.

Better to keep her mind on practicalities—what she was to say to him when she saw him. Or even *if* she saw him. Indeed, all her hopes were pinned upon the castle folk at least *attending* the Allantide fair, for even if they did not mix with the villagers, or play the games, she might at least see Lord Harry, and impose upon their old friendship enough to gift him with her enchanted apple. It might have some magic if it were only in his possession.

Aye. It was a lovely, diverting daydream: He would be drawn to her and take her apple and look at it—really look at it—as if he could somehow tell it was different from all the others. As if he could tell it was special. Special for *him*.

"Nessa Teague." His voice would be just as she remembered it—low and pleasing, easy and warm. And he would say her name the old-fashioned, Cornish way, with a sigh at the beginning: "Ah-nessa."

How she longed to hear him say it again.

"Nessa Teague?" A real, actual male voice drew her from

her reverie. "Is that really you hiding behind that bonnet? I thought I recognized you. You've grown even taller."

Oh, Saint Allan preserve her.

The man himself was there, in front of her, standing not two feet away, looking as amused and tall and handsome as ever in a bottle green coat. And he was looking at her as if she were a demented, too-tall looby who towered over all of the other female villagers and most of the menfolk.

"Harry," she answered faintly, working furiously to school her gaping stare into something more pleasant than demented. "Aye, 'tis I. How kind you are to remember."

"A kindness I must share with you, Nessa. 'Twas you I saw the other day in the street, was it not? With your mother? But I should have known you instantly, with those blue eyes and that wonderful smile."

Kind was far better than demented. And wonderful was—wonderful. "Thank you. Captain, isn't it now? How is your leg?"

The moment she spoke, Nessa felt heat blossom in her chest and creep up her neck. If her mother heard her, she would be aghast—Nessa ought to have said "injury" and not "leg" if she were going to talk of his body parts at all. Which she oughtn't. Because it was undoubtedly vulgar.

But Harry didn't seem to mind her ogling of his leg. "Still attached," he reported with a wry, pleased smile that pushed devastating dimples deep into his cheeks.

He was exactly as she had remembered him and yet different—he was taller, too, and his once lean shoulders were filled with a rangy power that came more from his stature than from any of the muscles that were sure to be flexing beneath the well-fitted coat. And though his eyes were as deep and warm a brown as ever, there was a depth to his gaze, a steadiness, that was new. As was the slight bump on the right side of the bridge of his nose, as if he'd been coshed across the face a time or two.

Poor beautiful Harry.

"And you are home, in England"—she had to swallow over the strange lump of heat and awkward yearning blocking up her throat—"for how long?"

"Until I can be declared fit enough to command a ship again without being a danger to myself or, more importantly, to others. It shouldn't be too long, so long as the shot stays embedded in my bone."

The thought that anything so ugly and evil could be embedded in such a beautiful young man was like a physical pain. Poor, wounded, brave Harry. "I am so sorry."

"Whatever for?" His quick smile snuck up one side of his mouth, as if his amusement were a surprise to him. "*You* didn't shoot me."

It was so like him—that marvelously mischievous sense of humor—that Nessa couldn't help her own reflexive smile. Which unfortunately gave way to stammering stupidity. "No, but... I reckon as you'd been shot on my behalf. I mean *our* behalf—the country and all, not me personally."

God help her, she was babbling. Just like the looby she swore she wouldn't be.

He laughed good-naturedly at her inanity. "I had reckoned the French shot me on behalf of Napoleon, but I don't think I would have minded half as much had I known I was being shot on your much more pleasant behalf."

It was just like him to try and make her feel less like an idiot. He always had, all those years ago when he had taken tuition from her father—those halcyon days when Papa had not objected to her joining his students at their studies.

But such days were long gone. Now she was meant to be an obedient, helpful young lady who was seen and not heard. To pay the servants and see that beds were changed, to arrange flowers for the altar and copy out her father's Sunday sermons in a clear hand.

But Harry looked as if sermons would be of little interest to him—he was eyeing the shifting crowd from under the brim of his hat, his gaze scanning faces, as if he were looking for someone. As if he were trying to find a friend.

She could be that friend. *And so much more.*

Nessa swallowed her nervous misgivings and forced her voice to an unstudied, casual tone. "Would you be so kind as to do me the favor of starting off the apple bobbing? It would be a grand thing to have Captain Lord Harry Beck take part in the Allantide fête." There, she had asked, even if her heart began thudding in her ears like the waves against the rocks along the coast.

"Ah, well—" He looked not exactly skeptical, but as if he were thinking of a way to get out of it. "Isn't this for the youngsters?"

"Aye." She cleared the lump of awkwardness from her throat. "But I need someone whom I know won't cheat to show the lads how it's properly done."

"Ah. I never cheat. Hands behind the back, isn't it?"

Nessa belatedly realized that his injury might make the balance of such a posture difficult. She'd let him do whatever he wanted if it meant he would take a chance with her apple. That's all she wanted, all she could ask for—this one chance.

"Oh, Harry. You can put your hands wherever you like."

CHAPTER 3

*T*HE MOMENT THE words were out of her mouth, heat swept across Nessa's face, so hot it all but left scorch marks upon her cheekbones. "I mean— I didn't mean—"

But Harry winked at her, just the way he used to do over the top of his Latin grammar book. "What interesting rules you've thought up, Nessa."

And just like that, she was shot through anew with all the hopeless, helpless, rapturous delight of her youthful infatuation—that peculiar, familiar ache that rose within her at the very mention of his name. At the sight of his face. At the thought of his pain.

He was *such* a man. Such a kind, thoughtful, beautiful man. The best man in all of England. In all the world. How had she survived twelve long years without once having the benefit and boon of his smile?

Not particularly well—Nessa could feel the accumulated years of loneliness press upon her like the preserved butterfly specimens in her father's study, pinned under glass.

But her reverie on a theme of all things Harry had kept

her from noticing the small knot of younger maidens from the village who had been standing out of Nessa's line of vision, darting forward to add their apples to the tub. They were all clearly hoping for the same as she—that handsome Lord Harry Beck would pick their apple and fall under *their* spell instead of hers.

And there was nothing Nessa could do to prevent it. She could only slip her own marked apple into the tub along with the rest and hope for the best. Hope that her tiny apple could hold a much larger enchantment. Hope her enchantment would work the strongest spell, so she could finally learn to release the breath she seemed to have been holding for twelve long years.

And then she really did hold her breath when Captain Lord Harry muttered what sounded like a very blue curse and simply plunged his head into the vat, chasing an apple all the way to the very bottom of the barrel. And then he came up with a splash and spray of water whipping off his hair and a bright red apple clenched between his straight, white teeth.

A cry of delight and a smattering of applause went up from the small crowd that had gathered, and Nessa clapped along with them. And then she stopped clapping. She stopped breathing.

Because the apple between his teeth was a small, perfectly rounded, perfectly polished Pendragon Red with her feathered arrow sign carved next to the stem—she could see it clear as day right next to his lip, where he held his prize in his teeth for all to see.

It had worked—the enchantment was as powerful as she ever might have hoped. More powerful that she ever might have dreamed.

Something more powerful than hope bloomed within her chest, hot and intoxicating and strong. The apple was hers. *He* would be hers.

All she had to do was step forward and tell him. Tell him the mark was hers. And then take a bite of the apple herself, twining the enchantment between them so he could fall in love with her. Finally, now and forever.

"La," someone breathed behind her. "But that's my apple, Lord Harry."

"No!" The denial leapt from her mouth just as Elowen Gannett stepped out of the small crowd with a look of perfect astonishment on her round, pink face.

"I beg your pardon. I did not know I oughtn't have taken it, Miss…?" Lord Harry smiled in his lovely, kind way and waited patiently for Elowen to supply her name.

But Elowen was too overcome with the excitement and improbability of the moment to speak sensibly. It was up to Nessa to salvage something of the truth from the moment, without savaging poor Elowen, whose only sin was being a trifle silly and dim, and rather too apt to jump to the wrong conclusion. "If my lord pleases, it's Elowen Gannett, sir. Her father is Squire Gannett, whose lands lie south of the village. Elowen, Lord Henry, Captain Beck."

"Sir." The dark-haired lass blinked her wide golden eyes, and curtseyed as if to the king himself. "You picked my apple."

"I think you might be mistaken, Elowen." Nessa tried to think of some kind way of showing her the mark, of correcting the simple mistake without being cruel.

But Elowen was well on her way to working herself into unreasoning raptures. "Aye, 'tis mine. 'Tis! He picked it, he did. You saw, didn't you?" Her voice rose, breathless with excitement, and her face flushed with hectic color as she turned to the onlookers in appeal. "You saw!"

She held out her hand. And there was nothing Nessa could do but watch helplessly as Harry handed the apple to Elowen, who instantly put the ripe red fruit right up to her own mouth, and sank her teeth into the soft flesh, biting off the little mark Nessa had so carefully carved into the skin, chewing and swallowing Nessa's last best hope.

Taking the enchantment all into herself. And destroying forever Nessa's bright chance at her dream.

~

HARRY LOOKED AT the pleasant young woman who stepped forward with expectation shining from her fair face and tried to keep the confusion from showing on his own. He had evidently chosen her apple, though just what such a choice signified, he was not exactly sure. He had only one strong boyhood memory of Allantide, which was of hot wax falling painfully into his eyes. And sweet, awkward, earnest Nessa Teague solemnly kissing his closed lids to take away the stinging pain.

Well, damn his eyes. However had he forgotten that?

A second memory followed hard on the first—of his father's cousin, the old Earl Banfield, inviting Harry up to the castle for tea and sticky cakes. Of the earl, sitting in his dark library and asking in his grave, calm manner about Harry's studies at the manse, and how he was getting on, and was vicar teaching him anything else besides mathematics? Harry remembered being unable to answer, because all he had been able to recall to mind that day had been Nessa and that strange, solemn, sweet kiss.

But Nessa Teague was not kissing him now—she was staring at the Gannett girl as if she had been struck dumb, like a concussed gunner gone mute in the heat of battle. What a strange thought—he was in peaceful, rural Cornwall, not on a frigate of war at sea. And Nessa Teague, however earnest, was far too fey for a gunner.

But whatever it was he was to do, Harry pledged himself

to submit to it manfully. He shook off the disappointment that this elfin Gannett girl was leading him away from tall, earnest Nessa, who mouthed, "Be careful," as he was led away.

Careful of what, he could not yet say, but he was grateful for the warning—the Gannett girl did seem somehow dangerous, though she did nothing but cling to his arm and tow him through the crowd. But unlike Nessa Teague, this girl looked as if she had…expectations.

He was clearly sailing in treacherous waters.

The instinct that had seen him safety through twelve years at the receiving end of French cannon had him politely but firmly detaching the attractive little barnacle from his person. "I'm afraid I can't give you my arm, Miss Gannett, as I've been injured." He wielded the compass-topped cane as if it were a weapon. Which it was—a weapon against presumption.

"Injured?" Miss Gannett blinked at him. "La, you'd think they'd take more care with a marquess' son."

Devil take him. Even without the uniform, he was known to be the Marquess of Halesworth's son—no wonder she found him, as they said in the navy, a ready target. "Miss Gannett, in the heat of battle, the cannonballs don't give a blazing damn whose son I am."

A shocked hand flew up to cover her petite, bee-stung lips. "Gracious me!"

Damn his eyes for a navy man. "I beg your pardon, Miss Gannett. Please forgive my rough manners. I've been at sea in the company of men too long."

His apology brought back her tremulous smile. "But you came back just in time for Allantide."

"Yes." He answered out of politeness, for he was distracted by the sight of Matthew Kent, milling through the crowd and looking only slightly less disreputable than the other day, wearing a woolen smock that marked him as fisherfolk. Kent briefly met Harry's eye, and then looked meaningfully at a portly fellow in an old-fashioned tricorn hat holding forth next to a cider keg.

"And your family, Miss Gannett? There was an old Squire Gannett in my youth who used to chase us out of his orchard if we dared to try and pilfer some windfalls, but it's been a number of years. Might he have been a relation?"

Miss Gannett appeared to have no head for ancestry. "That's my father, the Squire, there." She pointed to the garrulous man at the cider tap.

Excellent—the enemy was sighted. "I'd like to meet him, if I may?"

"Naturally," was Miss Gannett's happy response as she slipped through the circle of men surrounding her father. "Da, there's someone I want you to meet."

The squire looked down his red nose at Harry, even though he had to tip his head up to do so. "Oo's this then, Elly?"

"It's Lord Harry, from up the castle," Elowen Gannett supplied.

"Captain Harry Beck, Squire Gannett." Harry made his own introduction. He'd rather be known for the rank he'd earned for himself, rather than as one of the Marquess of Halesworth's spare sons. "A pleasure to meet you."

"You're the navy lad then?" The squire was a blunt country man, hard to impress. "Thought you'd'a been killed or summat."

"Very near to, Squire." Harry chose not to take exception, but to make himself as agreeable as Matthew Kent might like. He patted his thigh and gestured to his cane. "Those Frenchies tried their damnedest."

The assembled men broke into howling guffaws, but the

squire remained unimpressed. "And 'ow do you know our Elly, then?" he demanded.

"Oh, you'll never believe, Da." Elowen Gannett clutched her father's sleeve, eager to tell. "He bobbed for my apple that I slept with under my pillow last eve and marked with my own hand." She turned her beaming smile upon Harry. "And he picked it, in front of everyone. Everyone saw. And now he's mine. We're good as engaged."

CHAPTER 4

"DEVIL TAKE IT, no." The denial was out of Harry's mouth before Miss Gannett's high, excited voice had faded from hearing. And then there was silence—ominous silence as the crowd of men drew back as one.

"You sayin' you din't pick my girl's apple?" The words fell from the squire's lips like stones.

"No." Harry straightened his spine, consciously taking the stance he adopted on the quarterdeck of a ship—head high, eyes blazing. "I am not disputing my actions, only your very kind daughter's interpretation of them. I meant no disrespect—I mean none now—but I did not mean to offer marriage."

"Everyone knows what picking an Allantide apple means." The squire was adamant.

"Not everyone." Harry didn't. Or if he once had, he'd forgotten. Another casualty of living in harm's way for twelve long years—his memories were too crowded with dangerous episodes to admit more than a glimpse or two at the golden, tranquil years he'd had before.

Funny that his only memory of Allantide had been of solemn, earnest Nessa.

"Elly sez yer good as engaged, means yer engaged." The squire jutted his bulldog jaw close to Harry's. "If'n I decide to give mine approval."

Harry most devoutly hoped the squire would not give his approval. And since Harry was not the sort of man to simply sit and wait for the squire to withhold his approval, he began immediately to work to bring about such a profitable conclusion, though Harry wasn't one to lie, or act dishonorably, or allow himself to utter unkind things about the lady—who seemed to be taking his conversation with her father quite placidly, as if she had no doubt of their marriage coming to pass. "My father's approval would also be necessary."

It was not quite a lie—although Harry was only a spare son and, therefore, of lesser importance, he doubted his father would delight in allying himself with this blunt-spoken, potentially traitorous, country squire, who eyed Harry with the same animal inspection he might give his prized pig. "We'll see about that."

Harry promptly changed tack. "I don't suppose you'll want a crippled younger son without any influence or career prospects as a future son-in-law. I've done with the navy, you see." He held up the cane. "Invalided out. Nothing to do now but drink my way across the countryside." He smiled encouragingly to the fellow manning the cider tap.

"Don't want no drunk as mine son-in-law." The squire cast a quelling eye over both Harry and the tap man.

"No," Harry agreed cheerfully. "It seems no one does."

At that, the squire took up his daughter's arm and hustled her away like a prize heifer—or perhaps something more delicate, like a tender veal calf—and the squire's cronies suddenly found other things that required their attention, carefully taking the cider keg with them.

Pretend drunkenness had its drawbacks as well as its benefits.

Harry took up his cane and wandered indirectly in Matthew Kent's direction, beneath the shelter of a huge beech tree shading the sloping town common.

"You seem to be having an interesting morning," Kent observed when Harry moored up a few feet away from him against the stone fence ringing the common.

"Aye," Harry answered. "I seem to have shoaled myself rather badly on this rock coast of yours."

"Have a glass of ale and tell me your tale of woe."

"Good man." Harry accepted the pint Kent handed him. "It seems I've gone and gotten myself engaged, or some fool thing, without rightly knowing how."

"Well, if you don't know how it's done—" Kent's mouth twisted up in a wry smile. "But let me be the first to wish you happy."

"Don't be ridiculous. I can't possibly marry the girl. I *didn't* offer for her—I don't even know her. It's some fool thing to do with the apples—Allan apples. I'd forgotten."

"You've been away too long," Kent repeated.

"Aye." In more ways than he knew.

"So, who's the lucky lass?" Kent asked between sips at his own tankard. "Bound to be Nessa Teague, I reckon, or her alarmingly piquant sister."

"Nessa Teague?" The point of something perilously close to alarm harpooned its way through his chest, propelling him to his feet. "Why would you say that?"

"Saw you talking to her," Kent reasoned. "A family of only girls, opening a school to take in only boys. The vicar has to be mad. Or have something else in mind." Kent squinted at the clergyman in question, who was holding forth next to the cake tent. "But if not one of the Teague sisters, then whom?"

"My intended? Miss Elowen Gannett."

Kent let out a low whistle that ended on a chuckle. "Should'ha warned you about that one. Gormless but lethal, that girl. A pigeon ripe for the plucking, our Elly."

"Then why do I feel like the one who is in danger of being plucked?"

"Because you're not stupid. What did you think of the squire?"

"He's a blunt instrument," was Harry's opinion.

"I'd like you to find out more about him." Kent's gaze constantly roved over the assemblage, like a sailing master squinting his weather eye to the sky in expectation of rain.

Harry followed Kent's example, keeping his eyes on the common, even with unease clawing its way up his throat. "Is there no one else who knows the village and countryside, not to mention the coast, better than I?"

"No one else is at present engaged to the squire's daughter. You can be a blameless cipher coming round, asking your nosy questions for the purpose of the marriage settlements."

Harry's cravat strangled up as tight as a noose. "You can't think that I'll need to go so far as marriage settlements?"

"I hope not, for your sake." Harry could hear the smile in Kent's voice, even while he watched the common. "I don't imagine your father, the marquess, will take kindly to the squire, and vice versa."

"You're enjoying this."

"I am," Kent agreed. "And I'll enjoy it more when you find out everything you can about Squire Gannett, his business and his friends."

"You think he's your traitor?"

"Don't rightly know." Kent shifted, checking that their conversation wasn't being overheard. "And I don't rightly know how the treason plays in with the smuggling. The problem is that everyone is in on the trade, from the squire up the coast, down to the dimwitted mute who lives below the dock, and back up to the vicar's manse upon the village hill."

"Surely not the vicar?" What sort of man of God would be mixed up in a smuggling ring?

"The Reverend Mr. Teague likes his brandy."

True. Harry remembered the Reverend Teague retreating to his study for a medicinal snifter or two while his pupils had been meant to be conjugating their Latin and Greek verbs. Harry had always sought Nessa's help, and once the work had been done, the two of them had bolted for the outdoors. "So, what is to be done?"

"About the brandy? Nothing."

"And the treason?"

"Reacquaint yourself with the countryside, make friends in the village and with the squire—at least as much as you can bear. You tend to the land while I tend to the sea. I've a lugger at the quay—I'm a pilchard fisherman."

"How very Cornish."

"Don't let the quaintness blind you, Becks. It may look as pretty as a picture, but underneath all this whitewashed charm lie deadly serious secrets." Kent stood and downed the last of his beer. "Mind your back."

CHAPTER 5

ALL NESSA WANTED was to nurse her disappointment in private. She wanted to be out along the cliffs, where the wild sea wind would scour away the tears before they could even fall. Where she could think in private.

"Nessa?" Her father found her at the garden gate just as she was trying to slip out. "Ah, there you are. I'm sure you won't mind—I've a sermon for you to copy out. There's a good girl." He thrust the wad of foolscap into her hand and with a pat on her shoulder, started for the vestry without even waiting for an answer.

Which she gave anyway. "But where is Cods?" Cods the Curate, as they called him, was her father's assistant. By rights, he ought to have the responsibility for editing and copying out the thrice weekly sermons, as well as teaching in her father's schoolroom, not Nessa.

"*Mr.* Coddington is, no doubt, presently engaged with some other work of the parish this evening. God's work comes in many forms and at all hours, Nessa. You should know that."

Cods was *always* engaged in the work of the parish, if wandering around at all hours in a sort of incompetent haze while telling everyone how busy he was, qualified as work. He was late for every service, behind tempo on every hymn, and never, ever where he was most particularly needed to be.

Nessa thought Cods the most useless curate in all of God's creation. Especially when she had to do his work. Which was always. "Yes, Papa." She entered at the back of the house, dragging her disappointment with her.

"I saw you, you know."

Nessa paused at the bottom of the stairwell to find her younger sister, Tressa, peering through the balusters above.

With their Cornish names for first, second and third-born, the villagers had treated Kensa, Nessa and Tressa as a set piece—the Teague Sisters—interchangeable, one for the other.

Kensa had married a young gentleman farmer from Truro three years ago and was now the mother of two fine sons. But neither of the two remaining Teague Sisters looked to follow her matrimonial footsteps. To be fair, Tressa was only nineteen, and opportunities to meet eligible young gentlemen were few and far between—the fête notwithstanding. The war always seemed to take the best young men, like Lord Harry, from the village. Only the simple, the feeble, and the selfish remained. And the heirs, but no heir wanted a poor country vicar's second or third daughter for a wife.

"Saw me where?" Nessa asked. She had spent the rest of the afternoon minding the apple bobbing but didn't remember much of it—it was all blotted out by disbelief and disappointment. How could it all have gone so wrong?

"I saw you with Lord Harry."

"Mmm." Nessa made a noncommittal sound of assent to

cover the coiled skein of despair that snarled up her insides at the mere mention of his name.

"I *saw*, Nessa," Tressa insisted with quiet, subdued vehemence. "I saw him take *your* apple."

The ache that had only a moment ago been disappointment sharpened into something more cutting—it was one thing to have experienced such a devastating moment, but it was another thing entirely to know that someone, even a beloved sister, had witnessed the whole affair.

"Oh. That." Nessa retreated into silence until she could calm her wretched feelings. "But there is nothing to it, for it all came to naught."

"Only because you let Elly Gannett say it was hers."

The crushing weight of her disastrous day bore Nessa abruptly down to sit on the bottom step. "What was I supposed to do? Call her a liar? Let her make a fool of herself?" She shook her head. "That would have been cruel."

"Instead, you were cruel to yourself. You let her make a fool out of you."

"Oh, lord." Nessa took her head in her hands, as if it might hold her fragile dreams together. "No one could have known it was my apple. Everyone would have just assumed she was in the right."

"Not everyone." Tressa's tone grew softer and more sympathetic. "Not me. And when has daft Elly Gannett ever been in the right? Never. All anyone had to do was look at you, at your face, to see the truth."

"Oh, no." By now, the whole of the village might know of her stupid susceptibility.

Tressa reached a comforting hand through the balusters. "But I suppose no one else knows you like I do. You hid it well, really. Only I could tell how distressed you were. Because you're my sister."

They looked out for one another, the Teague girls did.

They may not have been made to the same pattern, but they were cut from the same strong cloth. The disappointment had hurt Nessa badly—it still hurt—but admitting it drew some of the venom from the sting. "Thank you."

"You're welcome. So, what are you going to do about it?"

"What can I do?" Nessa stood and smoothed down her skirts. "You saw—she ate the apple and took whatever fragile magic there was. If there ever was any at all. Which I should never have allowed myself to believe. It was wrong of me."

"I believe." Tressa's voice was strangely vehement. "And I think you need more magic. Better magic. Stronger magic than just a silly Allantide apple."

"Stronger?" Unease slid down Nessa's spine like a cold raindrop under her collar. "Tressa!" You don't mean…" Nessa lowered her voice to the merest whisper. "One of the witches? But that's just gossip and rumor. Isn't it?"

Bocka Morrow abounded with tales of secret meetings in the dark of the night. Most of the tales were true, especially about the smuggling. But there were other tales of the gypsies in the castle's woods telling dark fortunes and buying unwanted babies for half a crown. Tales of secret groups of women who met by the light of the blood moon, worshiping the old ways from the days before the word of Christ came to their island nation, celebrating the earth's own powers with fire and herbs and spells.

Rumor had it that charms and real enchantments, for good and for bad, could be had from one of these hedgerow hags—gypsies and witches alike—for a little as a penny.

And that was what she needed, wasn't it—charm? Because she had none of her own, not a drop. No captivating smile, no witty banter or flirtatious ways. No ability to say the right thing to captivate such a man as Captain Lord Harry Beck.

"Tressa, what do you really know about such things?"

"More than you, obviously." Tressa wasn't giving anything

away. "But if I were you, I would march myself down the cliff road to the Widow Pencombe with a shilling in my pocket to buy myself a real, honest to goodness love charm."

Nessa knew she ought to protest—ought to say something serious and corrective to her sister about flirting with the powers of evil, about their position in the community as daughters of the vicar, and about how their faith ought to be strong enough to carry them through without resorting to spells and charms.

But she didn't.

Because her prayers seemed to have fallen upon deaf ears or were perhaps worn out by familiarity. And because she wanted Harry Beck to love her more than she wanted anything else in this world.

CHAPTER 6

*H*ARRY ESCAPED THE oppressive atmosphere of the castle and did as Matthew Kent had asked, taking to the lanes to slowly reacquaint himself with the countryside and the landscape of smuggling.

The coast of Cornwall was a free trader's delight, fringed with high cliffs and hidden coves laced with flat, shingle beaches. Beaches that Harry could not, in his present state of injury, climb down to, damn the cramped ache in his leg.

But he could still see that the sheltered cove on the edge of Banfield lands, with high, formidable cliffs rising up like a paling, was perfect for smuggling brandy or lace, or tuns of cheap claret. Yet it was a long way to come to smuggle secrets—Harry would have thought the French would prefer to use the coast of Devon for closer proximity to the sources of such information in both Paris and London. Perhaps the quieter coast of Cornwall was held to be less closely watched, but they were watching now, weren't they—Harry on the land, and Matthew Kent on the sea.

Harry set his slow, cane-aided course up the serpentine path along the coast, counting the coves, searching for tell-tale signs of the places that smugglers might find useful to hide and store their cargoes until they could be moved inland. Exactly like the stone cottage hunched into the hillside ahead, as if it were trying to turn its back to the ever-blowing westerly wind.

The witch's cottage. The voice in his head was Nessa's, whispered in his ear as they had once lain hidden in the meadow on the other side of the stile.

And as if he had conjured her out of his memory, Nessa Teague came walking out of the wood into the field, her long loose stride scything through the tall grass like a benevolent force of nature. The wind made billowing sails of her skirts and hair, pulling the long, wheat-straight locks out of her tidy, vicar's daughter pins. The damp October air pinked her nose and cheeks, and she looked wild and fey and bloody marvelous.

Until she saw him and came to a complete stop in the middle of the meadow, all traces of easy confidence vanished as if the sun had shunted behind a cloud.

"Nessa." He raised his hand in greeting, willing her to move again. To move toward him.

She did so slowly, her footsteps far less confident through the long meadow grass. "Harry."

He liked how she still called him simply "Harry" without any my lording, or captaining. As if to her he was simply Harry and that was enough.

"Come out for a good long walk, have you?" He wanted to tease one of those solemn smiles out of her. "Or are you on your way to see the witch?"

"No," she answered almost too quickly, before she colored to the root of her sandy brown hair. On her face, wind-pinked spots turned a deeper red as she retreated into stammering silence for a moment before she finally spoke. "Why…would you think that?"

"Oh, I don't know." In the face of such pretty embarrassment, he decided not to tease her anymore. "I suppose I just wondered if the old witch still lived there."

"She does. I mean she's not a witch at all, really. Just a widow who's good with herbs—decoctions and such."

"And are you in need of such a nostrum?"

"No." She turned to face the cliffs, as if that had been her original destination. "Just out for a walk before it rained."

As afternoon rainstorms were a near daily occurrence along the coast in the fall, Harry decided to let the weather be his motivation as well. "I am doing the same, reacquainting myself with the area while I'm here. I'd love some company. Especially your company," he clarified. "We didn't get a chance to chat much at the fête."

"No." She looked down at her feet and then out to sea. "Well, you'd Elowen Gannett to talk to."

"Yes. Strange, that. Did you know about this Allantide apple nonsense?"

"Everyone does." She shrugged in apology. "It's a local tradition that the apple can pick your true love. Or true love will lead your love to the right apple. Or—" She retreated again into that stammering silence.

"But you don't believe in all that, do you?" he prompted. "Enchantments and true love?"

She tipped her head in the other direction, so the wind blew her hair across her fair face, obscuring his view. "Of course not. But it's been going on for ages—since the dark ages, to be more exact, when Roman Britain collapsed. The land and the people here have long memories."

She had always known her history in this casual fashion, as if it were a living thing for her and not just words out of a dusty book. "Doesn't your father feel compelled to preach against such paganism in his Sunday sermons?"

"Not him." She shook her head and smiled. "It's been this

way for as long as any of us can remember. He'd say it was good fun and that there's no harm in an apple—you have to believe to fall victim."

Harry didn't believe and he had somehow fallen victim, but that's not what she meant. "And you don't believe either, thank goodness, or people would have been feeding you apples all day."

She did not take it for the compliment he meant it to be. "No one tries to give apples to girls. It's only for the lads to do the choosing." She drew in a breath and steered the conversation into safer waters. "How's the leg?"

How like her to be so considerate. And now that he considered it, his leg didn't seem to ache so much. Perhaps it was the short rest. Or perhaps it was the easy camaraderie he felt with Nessa that relaxed him. "Coming along. Getting stronger but not strong enough for the cliffs, yet. This is the farthest I've come on one of my walks."

"You're a long way from the castle. Haven't they got a spare horse for you to ride?"

He laughed at the idea. "No. I've been at sea too long, I suppose—I'm a sailor, not a cavalryman—I've lost the knack for it. I'd probably fall off and break my other leg."

He amused her just as he had hoped—the ghost of a smile drifted across her face. "Not you, who used to race ponies across the sands at low tide?"

The memory came back to him in a gust—the streaking wind and the shrieking laughter, the pounding euphoria and the reckless joy. "And you?" Harry tilted his head down to get a better look at her face behind the veil of blowing hair. "Are you still racing ponies?"

"Me? No." Her smile was quick and bittersweet. "What a sight I would make with my long legs hanging down like ribbons below the pony's belly."

What a sight. Those long legs that could wrap around a

man and pull him tight. Those arms that could hold a man close—

Thought was instantly suspended as the blood vacated his brain and rushed straight to another, less governable, part of his body. And in his present somewhat weakened physical condition, his self-discipline was not equal to quashing a cockstand of surprisingly strong proportions.

Damn his eyes and the images that were now seared into his brain. But he could not damn the notion that sweet, funny Nessa Teague was a damnably attractive young woman.

"I think it would be charming."

She was not a girl for compliments. "I'm grown up now," she stated with a firm attempt at conviction. "Those days are gone."

"I liked those days." They had been some of the happiest he had known. "I liked that girl. She was rather extraordinary, as I recall. She used to tease me quite unmercifully. And beat me at those pony races."

This compliment was too obvious for her to avoid—she colored a vivid shade of pink. "That's because I knew the sands. And you didn't cheat."

"I still don't."

"No." Her shy smile was his reward. "You wouldn't."

But they were talking far too seriously if he hoped to charm her into telling him more about the village and its secretive ways. "Do you still sail?"

"Aye." She turned her face toward the sea. "I like the air and the wind."

He felt his smile broaden. There was something about being in her presence that made him comfortable and happy. "You'd have made a wonderful sailor."

She shook her head as if she were trying to ward off the compliment, but he could see her private pleasure by the light in her eyes. "What's it like out there," she finally asked, "on the open sea?"

Like breathing. Like living.

"It is my life." The entirety of his hopes and dreams and ambitions and life all packed into one sea chest of a career. "It is hard and lovely and rough and tough and the closest thing to true freedom I have ever felt, commanding a ship." And it was the only thing he could do. "It is what I do best."

She nodded, as if he had spoken sense. As if his voice had not taken on that edge of fervor. And desperation.

God, he missed it. He had missed a clear sense of purpose —but helping Kent was giving it back.

"You've been so far, while I've never been out of sight of the shore," Nessa mused, never taking her eyes from the wide expanse of blue-green water rolling endlessly toward the rocks below. "I wouldn't know my direction, or how to get on without orienting myself from the land."

"You'd get used to it. And you'd learn navigation—all those maths you helped pack into my brain, as a matter of fact." Her expressive face was just changeable and interesting as that ocean. "I don't think I ever could have conquered trigonometric projections without your assistance, so I must thank you for that."

A small, pleased smile pursed dimples into her cheeks. "You're welcome."

"And you know what else you could do that would make me eternally grateful?"

Her eyes met his in an instant, full of expectant trepidation. "No."

"Do you still have that little boat you used to keep in the harbor?"

"The sailing dory? Aye."

"Take me for a sail."

"What, today?" She put her face back into the wind. "It smells like it's coming on to storm."

A previously unknown piece of his internal rigging went taut, like a sail snapping full of wind. It was a physical feeling wonderfully close to pleasure. To desire. "I've never heard anyone say they could smell a storm. Feel it in their bones or see it in the sky, yes. I can often sense it in the air—the change in wind directions, the tufts of wind at different temperatures. But smell it? No."

A smile that seemed equal parts pleasure and embarrassment broke across her face like a summer dawn, rosy and brightening, before she tipped her head to hide behind her streaking hair.

"But tell me," he prompted before she could retreat into that stammering silence. "Describe to me this smell."

"Wet and heat mixed together in summer. Today, cold heated by brimstone. And a bit like geraniums."

His laugh was carried inland by the wind. "Geraniums?"

"We've some in the garden at the manse. You can give them a smell and tell me what you think."

"I think you're a rather extraordinary girl, Nessa Teague."

Her blush warmed her cheeks and put a rather lovely light in her wide blue eyes.

Funny, he'd never noticed their color before, her eyes. Or the marvelously variegated colors—autumn wheat and amber—of her long, straight hair that had escaped from her pins. "Say you'll take me sailing."

"All right." She raised her gaze and looked at him. He could see something that wasn't quite confidence, but certainly wasn't hesitation, warm the soft blue corners of those lovely eyes. "On the next fair day, I will."

CHAPTER 7

*C*APTAIN LORD HARRY Beck thought she was an extraordinary girl. And he had invited himself to go sailing with her on the next fine day.

Which, judging from the cloudless dawn sky outside her window, was today—last afternoon's rainstorm had blown all the clouds from the sky and the morning was so bright it nearly hurt her eyes. It was perfect for sailing.

And making Harry Beck fall in love with her.

Nessa was dressed before anyone else in the house was awake and was halfway across the garden, headed for the cliff path, when she was hailed from the adjacent churchyard.

"Ah, Miss Nessa. Just the person I was hoping to see."

It was Cods the Curate, the *last* person Nessa had been hoping to see. Especially as she could see a stack of notebooks tucked under his arm. "So sorry, Mr. Coddington"—Nessa raised her voice only loud enough to be heard, lest she wake the house—"but I must be off."

"Before Morningsong? And what could be so important, Miss Nessa"—his over-loud voice carried across the churchyard even more quickly than his long, spindly legs carried the rest of him—"to take you away from prayer? Would you ignore the call of the Lord?"

"Not ignoring," she countered, hurrying to unlatch the gate before he could reach her. Because it wasn't the Lord himself who was calling, but condescending Cods. "On my way to visit an ill parishioner." It wasn't exactly a lie—Harry wasn't ill, but he was injured. And he was, while he stayed at Castle Keyvnor, technically, a parishioner.

"You must tell me who it is," the impossibly tone-deaf curate pressed. "For *I* ought to visit as well."

Which was not at all a good idea. "Was there something you wanted, Mr. Coddington?"

"Ah. Yes," Cods said, as if he had just that moment thought of something and hadn't chased her down apurpose so he could practically pour the pile of notebooks into her arms before she could think to object or let the cursed things fall to the wet gravel path. "I'm sure you won't mind…Other duties prevent me…" He was already retreating, stepping away—"I know I can always count on you to do what's best, Miss Nessa…"—and hurrying off toward the church.

But not before she had her say.

"What's best would be for you to do your *bloody* job, Mr. Coddington." Nessa had never cursed out loud in her life, but she was *bloody well* tired of Cods thinking he could take advantage of her time and time again. And because Cods had already disappeared into the vestry, where he knew she could not follow.

"Bloody bother," she swore again.

"You're too nice for your own good, Nessa." Tressa's low voice came from the window above. "Why do you let him do this to you?"

She didn't mean to *let* Cods do anything. He just managed to do it—leave her holding the bag, or notebooks, or sermons. Every time. "Does that mean you're volunteering to correct these Latin grammars for me?" Nessa asked.

"Is that what he foisted upon you? Heavens no! You may be cursed with competence and a conscience, but I make no claim to the same. I'd make a hash of it."

"Bloody bother," Nessa repeated under her breath.

"That's the spirit." Tressa smiled down from the window. "First you curse, then you say *no*."

Her sister was right. Nessa stalked across the lawn to the glass paned doors that led to her father's study and before she could change her mind, tossed the notebooks inside. "Let Cods do it, the way he ought or take the blame." She closed the door. "I have an appointment to keep."

"Oh, brava, Nessa," Tressa cheered as Nessa marched toward the gate. "I begin to have hope for you yet."

Hope—what a strange thing it was. Two days ago, she had felt all hope had been lost, devoured in one single bite. And then she had met Harry along the cliff road yesterday and he had called her extraordinary. Today, her hope dared her to seize the day and find a way to make Captain Lord Harry Beck fall in love with her once and for all.

By going to the Widow Pencombe.

Nessa ran all the way to the cliffs, but once she had reached the cottage, she held back behind the shelter of gorse scrub, afraid to approach the shrouded figure bent over the smoking kettle hung over a fire. Of course, the iron kettle might have any sort of thing in it, from washing water to stew—Nessa had often seen such pots in the village and never been afraid.

And her need was stronger than the fear filling up her ears. No matter that her heart felt as if it would leap straight out of her body and bolt for the hedgerow like a frightened rabbit, Nessa forced herself to step forward. "Good day, Mistress."

The widow put a hand to her back to straighten up and regarded Nessa across the uneven grass. "Why, Nessa Teague." Her elbows jutted out, bristling like hedgehog spines. "Don't think I've ever seen you down my end of the path before. Did your mother send you?"

Heaven forfend her mother should ever find out about this venture. "No, Mistress."

"Or your father?"

Having her father find out would be only slightly better than her mother. "No, Mistress. No one knows I'm here."

"Ah, like that is it? Well, they won't hear it from me," the witch chuckled. "But there's many a soul as finds their way down here when things aren't going their way." She gave Nessa a long look-over, weighing her out like an undertaker. "Seen you about the town. And about the shore and coast and cliffs, walking. Powerful lot of walking you do, child."

The observation was mildly put and was true. "I like to walk."

"I reckon you do." The Widow Pencombe turned back to contemplate her kettle and its mysterious contents. "Powerful help to the restless, walking is."

Restless. She had never heard herself so described. People called her quiet, or shy, or even touched in the head, but never saw beyond that. Never wondered what she held back or kept in check in order to keep quietly to herself.

But it was as if the witch could see behind the locked door of her heart. "Aye, child. Powerful restless. Might even say troubled."

Nessa was sure her cheeks must be flaming, despite the cool chill of the autumn morn. She had never thought of herself as troubled. But she'd never been in love before. Not like this. "So can you help?"

"Help?" The widow narrowed her eyes and turned down the corners of her mouth as if she were weighing out the

39

decision, reckoning out the cost, like the ingredients of a potion. "Depends on what kind of help you think you need."

"I need help…in love." Nessa whispered the words so low, she could barely even hear herself over the wind.

But that same wind carried the words to the widow. "Aah. Love is it?"

Nessa nodded, glad that she'd gotten the worst of it over with. "Aye, Mistress."

"True love?" the widow probed.

"Aye." Of this, Nessa was sure. She had loved Harry Beck for as long as she could remember. Despite the years and the miles, no one had ever taken his place.

"With whom?"

His name seemed to stick in her throat—Nessa didn't want to expose him, or her susceptibility to anyone, even the witch, who might be the only one who could help her. "Lord Harry Beck."

"Aah." The old woman narrowed her eyes and nodded sagely. "He's a man for you. Why did you not try an Allan apple first?"

"I did." Nessa took a step forward, as if she might outpace her embarrassment. "But my apple failed."

The old woman's gray brows rose like gulls over her dark eyes. "Did it? That's bad luck. Or bad preparation."

"I did it just the way I ought," Nessa claimed. "Just like all the other girls said. And he took it—picked it right out, just as he ought."

"Then how did it fail?"

Fresh hurt and humiliation burned in her throat so that she could barely whisper. "Another girl said it was hers."

The Widow Pencombe made a hissing sound of deep disapproval. "That's powerful bad magic to claim an apple that weren't her own."

"I don't think Elowen meant to." Nessa felt compelled to

defend the poor girl. "I think she honestly thought it was hers." At least, she hoped so. But it had been *Nessa's* apple. "So, you see why I need a charm?"

"I do, child, I do. But charms are complicated, tricky things. Expensive. It will take a strong magic to counter such a wrong."

The word *magic* sent a shiver scratching up Nessa's spine. It sounded so heathen, so wrong. So expensive—she only had a shilling. "Just enough to counter the mistake and get things back aright, as they ought to be."

The widow nodded in agreement. "Aye, aye. But to counter your charm..." She narrowed her eyes to two coal-dark specks. "Did he bite the apple?"

"Aye." The soft crack as Harry had split the shiny skin with his perfectly white teeth echoed in her ears.

"That's good. That means he's got some of the Allantide magic—*your* magic—in him."

"But so does Elowen. She took the apple from him and bit into it, too, and ate my mark."

"Mmm. That's not good." The widow laid a long, work-roughened finger against her chin. "Have you a lock of his hair? No? A thread from his coat? A button? Anything? Nothing?"

Nessa had not thought to bring a talisman. "I didn't think to bring anything. Except my shilling." She held the coin out.

The old witch had it in her palm in the blink of an eye. "Well, that's the most important thing. I can make do with something of yours." She reached out and pulled a single strand of Nessa's long hair with a sharp tug. "That'll do nicely," the old woman muttered as she headed toward the squat, slant-roofed cottage. "You stay and stir the tallow. This may take some time."

Nessa stationed herself by the noxious pot and set herself to being useful—she tended the fire, rendered down the tallow, and when it was smooth and ready, began to dip the pairs of wicks to form the candles. By the time the widow returned, Nessa had nearly two dozen candles hanging off drying pegs.

The old woman stopped and stared. "Well, I'll say this for you Nessa Teague, the Devil must have to get up awfully early to try and get ahead of you."

Nessa warmed a little at the backhanded compliment. "Thank you, Mistress."

"You're a good girl, Nessa Teague. I can't say that about half the people who come knocking at my door looking for easy love. But I also can't promise that this charm will not fail you. I can only work to enhance what might lie between you, to make it steadfast and binding."

"Aye." Nessa would take what she could get and be happy.

"I must caution you, Nessa Teague, and ask you if you are sure you want to do this, because once you unstopper a charm, you cannot stop or correct or contain the way the love will go. What will happen, will happen. Do you understand?"

"Aye," Nessa answered.

"Are you ready?"

Nessa felt a sort of calm excitement, a sureness, a rightness come over her. "Aye."

"So be it." The widow put a small bundle wrapped in cloth in Nessa's hand. "Open it up." While Nessa did so, the witch unstoppered a vial and then poured the honey-like concoction over the cake. "This seed cake is now imbued with the charm of your desire. You must see that your true love eats it, and by your hand, do you see? And you must eat some, too. It is powerful magic, love is, so you must open your own heart to let the charm work its power. Do you understand?"

"Aye, Mistress. I'm to feed it to him and save a bit to eat myself."

"And in that order." She patted Nessa's hand, satisfied. "Now open your heart as well as your eyes, Nessa Teague. By the wings of your desire," she intoned. "By the generosity of the earth, and the goodness of your heart and soul and mind, may the lover and the beloved be one entwined, one heart, one mind. Let love be all that you can dare."

CHAPTER 8

NESSA STOWED THE seed cake safely in her pocket and headed for the quay, her head full of plans to quietly slip away with Harry with no one—certainly not her parents—the wiser. But her feelings were so fine, so elevated, so full of excitement and enthusiasm and expectation, that she took the steep lanes to the harbor at a giddy run, her arms windmilling to keep her balance as she pelted down the cobbles in a rush to arrive before Harry.

Only to find that he was waiting, leaning against the long stone jetty, and watching her ungainly flight with open amusement.

Nessa came to a breathless halt. "You're here."

"So I am." His smile was everything bright and welcoming. "I thought if I just stood here and concentrated, I might will you down the hill to meet me."

Nessa could feel her toes curl inside her boots—she was helpless in the face of such natural charm. "I came as soon as I could."

"Excellent." He turned to survey the harbor. "I have a bet

with myself to see if I remember which one is yours—the one with the red sails?"

"Aye. Well done. Is that a picnic?" She noticed a wicker hamper at his feet.

"It is, packed with care by Castle Keyvnor's diligent staff, so I've no idea of what's in it, only that we shall be very well provided for should I be able to convince you to run away to sea with me." He tipped his smiling face up to the sun. "For who knows when we may get another day so fine?"

Her heart was going to explode from pure, unadulterated happiness. There would never be a day so fine. Ever. "No convincing necessary."

"Shall we?"

She practically ran across the spit of shingle to the row of frape-moorings running out to deep posts, only belatedly mindful of his difficultly in navigating the sand with his bad leg and the hamper.

Because all the while her brain had been turning cartwheels of delight—a hamper! It was as if the magic were already working in her favor. The sooner she could invoke the full power of the charm, the better. Nessa immediately set to hauling in the mooring line.

"Allow me." He did not wait for permission but laid his hands right next to hers and lent his strength to pulling the looped line along the pulley. The boat fairly flew in to crunch its keel upon the pebbled sand.

Nessa felt herself all but vibrating from his closeness and the simple touch of his hand next to hers—she could feel his warmth spread from her nerveless fingers all the way to the tips of her curling toes. Gracious but the widow had clearly given her a powerful charm to already be working so well.

"The tarpaulin next," she instructed unnecessarily. As if a naval captain wouldn't know to untie the oiled canvas.

But Harry made no objection, immediately pitching in,

his long experience guiding him to the right task at the right time. It was no time at all before they were off the beach, with the sails up and the daggerboard down.

"You take the tiller," she offered immediately, swinging the hinged tiller his way. As giddy as she was, she might make some error of judgment and toss them headlong into the rocks. Best to sit quietly and let him do what he undoubtedly did better than she.

But he waved her off and settled into the sternsheets opposite, stretching out his injured leg. "I put myself in your more than capable hands."

Capable—the word doused some of her enthusiasm. That was what he thought of her—what everyone thought of her. Quiet, capable Nessa.

Not pretty. Not funny. And certainly not charming.

Still, she supposed there were worse things—she could be ugly or silly or incapable—and she had charm in her pocket, ready to be deployed.

Nessa tried to ignore the nervy anticipation gripping her belly and concentrate on steering. Few boats of the small fishing fleet remained in harbor—most had already put to sea at dawn on the outgoing tide—but she still had to be sharp to judge the flow of water through the narrow neck of water just right. But the sun was warm on her back as the cool autumn breeze filled the sails, her heart was full of hope, and her pocket was full of seed cake ready to bewitch Harry.

She felt a little bewitched herself, relaxed enough to take a lovely deep breath of the clean salt air. It was all going to be right as rain. The charm was already working its magic, for Harry was smiling, clearly happy with the excursion. "All these coves," he remarked. "It's no wonder there's so much smuggling."

Some of the wind—and hope—came out of her sails, though she reasoned there was nothing particularly probing about his comment. The free trade, as the villagers preferred to call it, was a rather open secret in Bocka Morrow—no one admitted to know anything about it, but everyone participated.

"I'm sorry—is it a taboo subject?" he asked. "Oughtn't I to know about such things?"

"No one is supposed to know about such things. But I suppose everyone does." And everyone included Harry. For all that he wasn't "one of them" as the villagers might say, he was a man of the world, a clever man of vast experience with human nature. And he'd lived in Bocka Morrow as a youth. Surely, he understood the way things were.

"Like that lugger there." He pointed across the water to a fishing boat anchored in the shelter of a shallow bay. "He's not netting pilchards, is he?" He shifted his seat to have a better look.

Nessa's disappointment took a shallow dive into unease. "On this coast, it doesn't pay to pry too closely into other people's business."

He turned to look at her as closely as she had him—too closely. But he came to his own conclusions anyway—he was too smart not to. "Is it as strong as ever, the free trade, despite the war?"

"I suppose." She shrugged, keeping her tone carefully noncommittal. "In some ways it's just as it's always been—just like-minded men on both sides of the channel wanting to trade their goods without interference. It's nothing to do with governments or the war."

"Oh, come now, Nessa," he chided, "you're cleverer than that. It has everything to do with the war. There is no escaping it."

While it was always nice to be thought clever—as opposed to stupid, anyway—it was uncomfortable to bear his scrutiny. She had thought of the war as something that happened far away—to him on his ship—not in the coves of Bocka Morrow. But now, under the weight of his straightforward, uncompromising gaze, she felt all the truth of his assertion. "I know."

He broke the moment, looking away. "I'd forgotten what this place is like—full of open secrets. I didn't even remember about the Allantide apples. Or maybe I never did realize the whole of their purpose. I suppose I was too young, before. I just thought it was a game." His dark brown eyes focused on her, as if he were trying to see through her—see more than she wanted to let people see. "You might have warned me, Nessa, before I ran afoul of the squire and Miss Gannett."

If the talk of the trade had not already sufficiently doused her aspirations, the mention of Elowen Gannett was like cold water on the fire of her hope. "I am sorry."

"So am I. What a strange man the squire must be—he seems to think nothing of his daughter engaging herself to marry a complete stranger on the strength of a single bobbed apple. I've never heard of such madness."

No more mad than pinning her hope on the strength of the seed cake in her pocket. The poor man—they were all of them fighting over him like a rag doll tussled between children, and not a man who had thoughts and hopes of his own. "What do you think I ought to do, Nessa?"

Look at me. See me. Want me.

"I don't know," she said, instead. It was an exquisitely painful test of character—she ached from holding all the love and adoration and longing inside her, but she gathered the courage that seemed stuck in her throat. "Do you not think you will marry her?"

He let out a short huff of disbelief. "Who could marry a person one doesn't even know? And what kind of person relies upon an apple to decide their fate for them?"

The same sort of person who relied upon a seed cake—a lonely person, a desperate person. A person just like her.

"No thinking person," she offered.

"Exactly!" His relief was palpable. "How like you to understand that, Nessa."

"Aye," she agreed because she couldn't *not* agree. "One must think."

"And I think I'd like a closer look at that lugger. Prepare to come about." Harry wrapped his hand over hers to steer the dory into Black Cove, and if the feel of the warm strength of his fingers were not enough to send her thoughts scattering to the wind, the change in direction brought her sliding up tight to his side.

She was overwhelmed by his nearness, by the heat of his body, the scent of his soap and starch of his linen.

He was not similarly affected. "All right there?" he asked with a bright smile.

Up close, his teeth were impossibly white and even. Up close, he was impossibly handsome and fine. Almost too fine for the likes of her.

But the charm must have been exerting its power, because there she was, cozied up next to handsome, fine Harry Beck. "Aye. All to rights."

She felt her face grow warm with the loveliness of it all and forced herself to marshal her wits enough to turn and raise a hand of acknowledgment as they approached the lugger. "They'll know it's me," she explained. "There's precious little privacy in a village so small." She would have a lot of explaining to do this evening, when she got home—in Bocka Morrow word of a person's doings could travel faster than stink.

"Well, that's a pickle." Harry's smile slid to one corner of his mouth, pressing that perfect dimple deep into his cheek.

"A man doesn't like to be spied on while he's trying to woo a girl."

Nessa's breath bottled up hot and airless in her chest. She could barely breathe the word out. "Woo?"

"Ah, Nessa." His voice was low and quiet and sure. "You don't think I've packed a picnic and brought you all the way out here just so I could spy on idle pilchard fishermen, do you?"

CHAPTER 9

HARRY WASN'T QUITE sure what came over him, but whatever it was, it was bloody marvelous. Beneath his fingers, he could feel the fine strength in her capable hands, the heat of her sun-warmed skin.

It was a curious thing, this sudden need—this compulsion—to touch her. But he supposed he had always been curious about long, tall Nessa Teague and her solemn smiles. It was like a low fire he had banked within, only needing a fine breeze to blow into flame.

What had she been doing for the twelve years he had spent tempting fate in front of French cannon? Why had she not yet married? When had she become so particularly, singularly beautiful?

She was, after all these years, newly irresistible.

And he wanted nothing more than to indulge his curiosity.

At his question, she had gone still, staring at his hand, with her straight dark brows pleating into one emphatic line. But she didn't remove her hand. Or his.

Harry could only hope she felt the same strange magic as he. Hope she was as utterly enchanted.

And the look she gave him—all breathless wonder—was his answer and reward. The lugger, the trade, and even the treason were entirely forgotten in the simple but consuming pleasure of her solemn regard.

Beneath his fingers he could feel the febrile fluttering of her pulse. He could hear the shoaling cadence of her breath and see the darkening of her eyes as she lifted her gaze to his. Was this what it was like—attraction, infatuation, and perhaps even love?

Lust he had certainly felt before, but not this. Not this strange feeling that stirred his body and his mind all at the same time, like a warm winter toddy swirling down his veins. Not this care and need combined into something hot and urgent and necessary.

"Nessa," he said again, because it seemed the only word he was capable of saying when she looked at him like that—as if he were the sun and she were a moor flower, stretching towards his rays.

He felt drawn to her as well, drawn by need and hope and something hovering at the edge of his mind urging him toward her. He did so slowly, giving her all the time in the world to pull back or change her mind.

She did not—she stayed still, watching him come closer and closer with those wide, unblinking eyes. His gaze fell to her mouth, to the plush pillow of her lower lip, plum colored and parted below the perfect scoop of the upper.

It was madness—a necessary madness—to kiss her. But he could not stop. He didn't want to stop.

Another steady beat of his heart, another inch closer to the invitation of her barely parted lips. Another breath, and he had closed the space between them. He was falling under the spell of her body, enchanted by the light, innocent fragrance of primrose radiating from her skin, mixing with the homey starch of her linen. And just the thought of her linen, of the lawn chemise hidden behind layers of practical, sturdy fabric and stays—boned and laced and holding her like an embrace—brought him to a nearly painful state of attraction.

Harry angled his head to meet her lips, trying to be careful, trying to make his mouth brush gently against hers, but she was so soft and giving and sweet he felt upended, as if the boat were rolling endlessly over the crest of a wave.

He dipped his head and came again, catching her lower lip between his, pressing his mouth more intimately to hers. Her eyes slid shut, and her straight brows drew together in a frown, not of displeasure—for she did not draw back—but a sort of disbelieving wonder, as if it were almost too good to be true. As if she were concentrating on this alone—this kiss, this astonishing feel of their lips meeting for the first time.

And then she sighed, a sound so romantic and delicious and erotic, he nearly groaned in response. "Ah, Nessa."

His arm slid around her back to hold her steady and sure while—

He was flung away from her as if by a ghost's hand, shot forward, out of the sternsheets. But so was she, landing atop him in a tangled heap of skirts and petticoats on the hard, raised grating in the well of the boat. Harry rolled, instinctively sheltering Nessa with his body, protecting her from—

Nothing.

The alarm that had flashed through his blood like lit gunpowder fizzled out. They were shoaled—he had shoaled them.

"Oh, Devil take me." Air sucked back into his chest. "I've run us aground." He had been so completely taken up with kissing Nessa Teague that he had forgotten his direction and his training and his experience so far as to shoal the vessel against the strand.

What an ass he was.

Harry shifted off her reluctantly. The feel of her long, lithe body beneath his—

"Are you all to rights?" His hands cradled her skull, turning her face up to his. "Are you hurt from the fall?" Or from the weight of his thirteen plus stone crushing her into the floorboards?

"Aye. I'm all right." Her hands were righting her clothing, pushing herself upright, and gingerly exploring the back of her head where he had slammed her to the floorboards.

A complete and utter ass. "Are you sure?"

At her nod, he made a cursory inspection and found that, by the Devil's own luck, the dory had safely beached on the thin strip of shingle bracketed by monstrously large rocks.

"You will think me the most incompetent Royal Navy captain there is." He had done the reputation of the senior service no favors this day. "Promise me you won't tell a soul I ran a dory aground or they'll never let me command anything bigger again."

She gave him a small, sweet smile. "I promise. Your secret is safe with me."

"Ah, Nessa." He couldn't stop himself from brushing a wayward strand of fine hair off her face. "You always did look like the sort of girl who could keep a secret."

Her smile faded, like a wave ebbing away from the shore. Her gaze shifted back to the lugger, reminding him of where they were and what he was supposed to be doing before he had let himself become enchanted by the loveliness that was her. "This is Black Cove," she said. "Named for a famous wreck on this very strand. Many's the man who's come to grief here."

The lighthearted charm of the moment evaporated into

the crystalline air. She certainly did have secrets. And he would have to pry each and every one of them out of her.

"SHALL WE HAVE our picnic here in the boat or would you prefer the strand?"

Nessa thought it best to move—to try and find her balance. The kiss made her feel conscious enough, but her head was ringing like the inside of a church bell.

"Above." Nearer the base of the cliff they would be out of the wind, out of sight of the prying eyes of the lugger, and out of the dory, which felt too small to hold all the conflicting feelings coursing through her mind and body. "They say the strand is haunted."

She purposefully turned her attention away from hauntings and kisses to setting out the meal—cold roasted chicken accompanied by wine and cheese, bread and fruit served on nested porcelain plates with the Castle Keyvnor crest painted in gold. Nessa had never eaten off anything so fine, let alone a picnic meal in Black Cove.

"Do you remember when you used to help me raid the manse's larder, stealing bread and whole wheels of cheese?" he asked.

She remembered everything about Harry, every single minute, each treasured moment. "You were always so hungry."

"I was. But not as hungry as I learned to be in the navy."

"Oh, I am sorry." She offered him the first thing to hand—a piece of fruit. "You can eat your fill today."

"Thank you, but I think I'll stay away from Cornish apples today."

Nessa felt her face flame. "Perhaps not an apple. Perhaps…"

She rummaged blindly in the hamper until it came to her—this was the moment. This was her chance to give him the charm. To make him love her.

"Perhaps..." Her heart squeezed the breath from her chest.

"Come, Nessa." He smiled in that easy, open way, full of encouragement and charm. "I hope we are friends enough that we can speak freely to one another and say what we are thinking."

"Friends," she repeated. "Aye. Yes, friends." It was as if the word itself was taunting her. She drew the small cloth-wrapped bundle from her pocket. "I made you something. I'm afraid it's awfully squished from our rather abrupt landing. But I hoped... That is, if you like seed cake?"

He reached out to take the cake from her hand. "Did you? How sweet."

She steadied herself, really she tried, but her hand was shaking so badly she nearly dropped the sad lumpen little cake before he could take it.

"Are you sure you're all right, Nessa?" He dipped his head down to look into her eyes. "Did you hit your head when we ran aground?"

She had done, but she knew it was the pounding of her heart, hammering away in her chest like a blacksmith's bellows that made her feel so lightheaded. "I don't think so. But perhaps a little cake will help." She broke off her small bit, but then rather thrust it at him so that he had no choice but to take it from her hand.

But he only took a bite of the thing and grimaced.

"It's awful. Is it awful?" She didn't wait for his answer but tasted it herself—it was dry and bitter, and not at all as a seedcake ought to be. "Oh, I am so sorry." Her own mouth twisted with displeasure. "It *is* awful."

"It is," he admitted. "But I am glad, for I have finally found something that capable Nessa Teague, who can sail, and run a fête, and teach mathematics, and regularly rewrite her father's Sunday sermons, cannot do—she cannot bake a competent cake."

"No." Mortified heat singed her neck and across her cheek, even as she laughed at herself. Because he praised her, at least a little, as he teased. And he had eaten some of the cake. Nessa took another bitter bite on the general theory that the more charm they shared, the better.

It was still awful. "What do you suppose it's lacking? What did I forget?"

"Sugar, I should think." He laughed with her. "Even though it is a luxury to which I have grown unaccustomed aboard ship, I still miss it in a cake."

"But you are a captain now, with your own ship, and a respectable fortune of your own in prize monies—surely you can afford sugar when you sail?"

"You know the worth of my fortune, do you?"

"No," Nessa stammered. The charm was clearly no antidote to embarrassment. "I mean—that is, I only know what was written in the newspapers or what people said."

"Ah." He accepted her explanation gracefully, with an easy smile. "Nice to know you were thinking of me."

She had. Constantly. She thought of little else. "I should think it a wonderful life, seeing the world—all the places and peoples, all so different."

"You think you should like to be a Royal Navy captain and command a ship full of rowdy, stinking men?" His brows rose in disbelief over his smile.

"No, for that would be impossible." She was not so much of a dreamer that she wanted the impossible. "But I should like to take at least one adventure in my life and see at least some of the world, instead of living always in the same hidebound place all my life."

"Bocka Morrow does not seem such a bad place to live. In fact, it doesn't seem hidebound today, but exciting and beautiful."

He was going to kiss her again. She knew it from the light in his eyes and the way his gaze fell to her mouth, just as it had the first time—that first awkward, lovely, blissful moment when his lips had pressed themselves so firmly to hers. So blissful that her whole heart was squeezing itself into a quivering pudding from wanting him to kiss her again.

But this time, she would keep her eyes open. This time, she would watch his extraordinary gold-flecked brown eyes darken and draw nearer. So near she could count the number of his lashes and marvel at the difference in texture between his rougher cheek with his whiskers just below the skin, and the taut smoothness of his lips, like wild strawberries from the hedgerows.

His lips settled upon hers tentatively, gently teasing her into joining him in this feast of taste and texture and scent and warmth and intoxicating delight.

Not that she had ever been intoxicated—her mother did not approve of her girls taking wine at dinner, nor even a sip of the elderberry cordial she saved for special occasions. But Harry's kiss made her feel giddy and ecstatic, as if she couldn't possibly ever get enough of his lips pressed so intimately against hers.

She melted into him, pressing herself against his chest and looping her hands about his neck. This was a kiss with no hiding, no modesty—nothing but unfurling pleasure. Their mouths met, but she felt the kiss everywhere, from her lips to her hands and even the soles of her feet, which seemed to tingle with delight and longing.

And then she felt his hand, slow and sure, sliding around from her back to her side. His thumb traced the line of her stays where they scooped below her arm and his palm gently covered the round of her breast.

The pressure and weight and warmth of his hand were enough to penetrate the layers of cloak and fabric and stays and chemise, so that her nipple tightened with a pain that was almost pleasure. Almost enough pleasure to keep herself from drawing back, out of his arms, and away from his lips. But not enough to override the scruples that went deeper than the layers of clothes.

"Too much?" he whispered against her temple.

Too much and not enough, but far too much to understand in a single moment. She did not know if she had thrown herself at him or he had thrown himself at her. Perhaps they both had. Perhaps the seed cake, however bitter, had thrown them together. Or perhaps not.

Because Harry was no longer looking at her. He was looking over her shoulder into Black Cove, where the receding tide revealed a widening fissure in the rock.

"Devil take me. Is that a smuggling cave?"

CHAPTER 10

*H*ARRY FLATTENED HIMSELF on the picnic blanket, wishing for his spyglass. There was a small collapsing glass at the bottom of his trunk up at Castle Keyvnor. And speaking of which— "Is this Banfield land?"

"No." Nessa's voice was as thin and strained as frayed rigging. She was nervously eyeing the lugger, still idly anchored in the deepest part of the cove. "That's Black Cave. It's said to be haunted by the ghost of the man who wrecked his ship and all his crew in this cove. But the coast is riddled with such caves," she said, as if it might underplay the importance of this particular one. As if she felt disloyal for providing him with any information at all.

He felt a sharp pang of conscience pierce the armor of his duty. But finding the traitor—or traitors, for such endeavors were rarely the work of only one man—was more important than any misapprehension or misplaced loyalty she might feel. The cave might house treason. "Then whose land is it?"

She took a long moment to answer, still reluctant to spill local secrets. "Hollybrook Park, Viscount Lynwood's estate. It abuts Castle Keyvnor's park."

The Lynwood name fell like a hot cinder into Harry's ears, lighting him up—his sister had mentioned something about Lynwood or Hollybrook. Or something. Harry hadn't paid much attention—his mind had been on their traitor. "Banfield and Lynwood—were they on good terms?"

"No," Nessa's glance slid to the emerging cave. "The earl and the viscount were said to be at odds, even mortal enemies, though it was only village rumor." She sat up, brushing the crumbs of their meal from her skirts. "I think I must go."

"No." The denial sprang from his lips too quickly. There was clearly more she was not telling. "Were Banfield and Lynwood rivals in the smuggling?"

"No." She hesitated. "Banfield forbade any smuggling on his land."

Harry tried to cast his mind back twelve years, to that singular invitation to tea at the castle. To the earl's pointed questions about the course of studies at Reverend Teague's school and what else Harry had gotten up to. Could the earl have been suspicious about the reverend's connection to the smuggling even then?

Was that why Nessa was so uncomfortable now? "I must go," she insisted. "I must— There are sermons that need copying."

"Surely the sermons can wait. We were having such a lovely day—"

"Aye." The word sounded as though it had been wrenched from her. "We were."

It was accusation enough for Harry to know he had been too eager, both about the kissing and about the smuggling—he had rushed them both. "I'll see you home," he offered. He could make amends on the sail back to the harbor, where he could find Kent and give him the information about the cave on Lynwood lands. It made sense that one of the major landholders in the district was complicit in the free trade, because—

"Nessa?"

He was alone—while he had been making his plots and plans, Nessa had scrambled up the rough, steep incline toward the clifftop, where his lame leg would not allow him to follow. "Nessa!"

She stopped abruptly and looked at the lugger. And then back at him with a painful mix of accusation and plea written across her face, as if she could not believe how stupid he was to be shouting her name across the clifftops. As if she were utterly devastated to realize he would use her so.

A bilious mixture of shame and guilt swirled its sour way into his gut. Damn him for an ass. He would make it up to her. Just as soon as he told Kent about this Black Cave, and investigated it, and found his traitor.

But it was many hours later before Harry made it back to the village harbor, and found Kent sitting on the bench in front of the Crown & Anchor when Harry finally made his way back to Bocka Morrow's quay.

"Afternoon," Kent tipped his battered hat as if Harry were a stranger. "Have a nice sail, sir?"

Harry took the other end of the bench and pitched his voice low, though no one was around to overhear. "Found a cave a few miles up the coast on Hollybrook Park land, just over the boundary from Castle Keyvnor's estate. There was a lugger anchored there for the better part of the morning. They stopped doing whatever it was they were doing while we were there, but—"

"We?"

"A friend took me out in their boat."

"A friend? Is that what we're calling young women these days? Careful your betrothed doesn't find out."

Harry chose to ignore Kent's gibing tone. "The *Rowena*, it was. Know her?"

"She's Arthur Morgan's. He lives at the south end of the village here. Not the sort to have a large share of a cargo—modest man."

"He was anchored in Black Cove for the better part of the day while the tide ran out. And they didn't make any show of setting out their ship's boats for a pilchard catch. I'm fairly certain they could identify me. Nessa said they'd have a glass on us—"

"*Nessa* said?" Kent's head went back, absorbing that information as if he were deflecting a blow. "Be careful with the intriguing Teague girls, Becks."

"What do you mean?" Was Kent implying that Nessa not only knew far more than she had let on, but that she might somehow be involved?

"I mean take care," was Kent's cryptic response. "Everywhere I look in this business, I see the vicar or his family."

Everywhere Harry had looked, he'd seen Nessa. Nessa flying down the hill, eager to join him. Nessa practically throwing herself at him to distract him from the lugger. Nessa.

Damn his eyes. "We'll head back to that cove tonight. I calculate the tide will be out for another six hours—

"No. You leave Black Cove to me—as you said, they might recognize you from your sail today." Kent made his decision. "While Black Cove is in play to the north, I need you to head south and tend to your betrothed."

The guilty punch in his gut was all for Nessa, and the liberties he had taken. "Nessa and I are not betrothed."

"I was speaking of Elowen Gannett, Becks." Kent spoke with slow deliberation, as if he shouldn't have to remind Harry of his precarious situation with another village daughter. "And her father, the squire, who may or may not have his finger in this pie. Actually, I know he must have his finger in the pie, but I want to know how deep."

Harry swallowed down the bitter disappointment about Nessa. "I'll try to find out."

"Use your charm, Becks," Kent advised. "You're a handsome toff—an earl's son. I reckon you can charm Elowen Gannett into letting you right through the squire's front door."

CHAPTER 11

NESSA COULD NOT tell if the heat pooling behind her eyes were tears of frustration or mortification. The charm had failed. Or she had failed the charm. Not that it mattered—either way, she felt wretched.

The day had been a miserable, bitter failure. Mostly.

Because there had also been that kiss.

Or more properly—or improperly—kisses, plural. A long, lovely series of kisses that made her breath catch and her belly sigh with pleasure even now, when she knew that Harry was more interested in the free trade and their caves than in her.

Her solitary path along the line of the cliffs toward home brought her near enough to the witch's cottage that she could not avoid the widow, who stood in her patchy, overgrown garden with her hands on her hips as if she had been watching and waiting for Nessa to arrive.

"Mistress," Nessa greeted her, for there was no possibility of passing without doing so.

"Well?" The old woman beckoned her nearer. "Are you going to tell me?"

Nessa didn't want to—it mortified her that anyone might know of her disappointment. But of all the people in Bocka Morrow, perhaps the Widow Pencombe was the one person she might tell without worry that it would be bruited across the village common. "It failed," Nessa admitted before amending her words. "*I* failed."

"What do you mean?" The old woman grew indignant. "Did he not make love to you? For you've the look of a girl who's been kissed long and well—your lips are swollen and your cheek are chafed pink with the fellow's rough skin and whiskers."

Nessa could feel her face flame pinker still. "Yes, he did kiss me."

"Aha!" The witch clapped her hands in glee. "It was a rare, strong charm I made you."

"Yes, but..."

"But what?"

"He didn't eat it all. He didn't like it, the seed cake. It was rather...bitter."

"Ha!" The old woman cackled. "You didn't think true love was going to go down easy, did you? You didn't think you could take the sweet without the bitter?"

Nessa *had* hoped so. Even if she hadn't thought it would be easy, she never thought true love would be so hard.

"You young lovers," the widow complained. "In your own way more often than not. Stop fretting and worrying about what will happen next—it will all come out with the turn of the moon. What is meant to be is meant to be—the charm can only enhance what is already there."

Nessa hoped there was something there—something beyond curiosity about the smuggling. She turned for home, already making a mental list of all the things she would need to do before supper to keep from the scolding that was undoubtedly waiting for her.

"Miss Nessa," a voice from the other side of the hedgerow interrupted her thoughts.

It was Cods, the inconvenient curate, hurrying himself away from some unwanted task. "Do I perceive that you've just come from the witch's house?"

As Nessa's path clearly came directly from the cottage, there was no point in lying. "I have come from the Widow Pencombe's."

Cods was instantly all dire apprehension. "You must take care, Miss Nessa. The woman is—"

"Kind. And skilled with herbs," Nessa finished for him.

"If you are in need of such skill," he countered, "why do you not visit the apothecary in the village?"

Nessa almost smiled. Clearly Cods had not yet arrived at the realization that the apothecary was run by women very much like the widow, including her niece, Brighid. "Because the Widow Pencombe is poor and has a far greater need of my pennies than the apothecary."

"She has no claim on your charity," Cods condescended to instruct. "She does not attend divine services—she is a nonbeliever. Her sort should have been banished from this village long ago."

"Thank you, Mister Coddington." In her present state of disappointment, Nessa did not want to parse the meaning or necessity of charity with the curate. "But I would rather err on the side of generosity."

Cods looked down the length of his nose at her—even though they were of a height and he had to tip his head back to do so. "I had not thought you so ungrateful, Miss Nessa, as to resent a correction from a person with a far greater experience of the world than you. My advice was kindly meant."

"Mr. Coddington." Nessa drew herself up stiffly, or as stiffly as possible whilst she was so filled with frustration and disappointment, and probably *had* hit her head harder than was good for her. "If I have no great experience of the world, perhaps it is because I am forced to copy out sermons when I could be doing something more edifying, if only my father's curate made time to do his own job."

Her salvo delivered, Nessa stalked off in a flurry of unhappy, burning indignation. But the ridiculous, stupid man did not have the consideration to wait a moment before resuming his own journey toward the manse—he dogged her footsteps all the way home.

It was no wonder she was called into her father's study within minutes after her arrival. "Oh, Nessa. There you are," her father said, as if he happened upon her purely by accident, as if seeing her were always surprise. "Mr. Coddington mentioned that he saw you out with young Lord Harry Beck."

Damn Cods and his nosy, always-in-the-wrong-spot-where-he-was-not-wanted ways—he had seen even more than he had let on. "He is Captain Beck now, Papa. You must be very proud of your former student—he has done very well for himself in his career."

Her father was momentarily diverted. "Yes. All those maths he was so very good at came in handy in navigation." He turned to stare out the window and stroke his chin in contemplation, as if he were trying to think of what next to say. "You seem to take a great interest in young Lord Harry."

"Do I?" She refused to feel guilty. "He is a friend of long standing. As are many of your current and former students."

"Do you go sailing in Black Cove with all my former students?"

"No. But I used to do." Before her father had stopped her from most of the teaching—and left her to correcting the improperly taught lessons. "And Captain Beck is just passing a few days' time in the parish while his father visits Castle Keyvnor."

"Yes, the reading of the old earl's will. I imagine I'll go up myself on the day. I've had a notice there's a small bequest for the church's roofing fund. But that is neither here nor there." He pinned Nessa with a look. "I think it best if you watch him—use his fascination for you once again."

Alarm spread like pinpricks along her skin. "Again?"

"Yes. Keep him out of the way and away from the trade. Just as you used to do."

Nessa felt as if she had been doused by a cold bucket of shame—she did not know when she had felt so thoroughly and utterly manipulated.

"Watch him," her father repeated. "But no more—don't do anything stupid like pine after the man, Nessa. That would never do." Her father shook his head as if the very idea were preposterous.

Nessa had to agree. It was not only preposterous, but dangerous. Because she knew exactly what pining after Captain Lord Harry Beck had already led to.

CHAPTER 12

*H*ARRY TRAVELED TO Gannett Hall in his father's crested coach to make a suitably impressive entrance. He would have to sail a fine course, ingratiating himself enough to gain the squire's confidence, while holding off any agreement to an actual betrothal. Deep seas, indeed. Devil take him if he didn't end up dashed against the rocks.

Miss Gannett greeted him at the door of the ancient Hall with a low, melting curtsey. "Welcome, my lord. I'm sure it's not so fine as the castle, though it is nearly so old."

She conducted him into the vaulted Tudor interior with a nervous pride that instantly made Harry feel even more guilty at so knowingly using another female.

What had Kent called her—gormless? Poor girl.

"It is a very handsome building, Miss Gannett," he enthused. "Quite ship-like, with all the wonderful carved wood, but almost too fine for a rough sailor like me."

"But you're not rough at all," she exclaimed, all coy protest, "being a marquess' son."

Gormless but lethal—Harry would do well to remember

Kent's exact words. "I am the marquess' second son, Miss Gannett, not his heir. I stand to inherit nothing of substance from my father's estate."

"La." She waved the concern away. "That is of no account, for I *am* the heir, or rather, the heiress. My father has no other children—and thankfully no inclination to get a new wife—so there is no one to inherit but me."

This, Harry knew, was meant to entice him into considering her and the engagement in a more profitable light. And if he were a different man, such an alliance might have had its advantages and appeal.

But he was not a different man—he was a man committed to duty.

And a man who was already in love with another.

The thought pierced him like a single bullet from a sharpshooter—he was in love with Nessa Teague. He was in love with her solemn smiles and fey kisses, her quiet humor and happy good sense, and her wide blue eyes that looked at his so levelly.

If only he had bitten *her* apple and entangled himself with *her* in an engagement, he would not find himself in such a tenuous, impossible position.

If only her father were not entangled in treason.

The sobering thought firmed his purpose.

"My lord?" Elowen Gannett conducted him to the other end of the hall, where the Squire stood gazing into the low fire. "You'll remember my father, Squire Gannett. Da, Lord Harry Beck, as you'll remember from the fête."

"Squire Gannett." Harry bowed properly before extending his hand, which the Squire chose not to take. "Captain Beck, at your service."

"Put off our supper to have you to 'dinner'," the squire growled by way of greeting. "But you're here, so let us eat before my haunch of beef is ruint."

"There, there, Da." Elowen patted her father's arm. "The haunch is quite safe. Mrs. Blackstone has it all in hand."

Her father thumped into his chair at the head of the carved Tudor table set with covered dishes. "Don't like my schedule disrupted," the squire groused. "I'm no man of leisure to be putting off my supper till all hours of the night. Time and tide wait for no man."

"My apologies, sir," Harry said in an attempt to be a sympathetic guest, and because he, more than many, understood the absolute tyranny of the tide. "Do you have sailing or fishing interests, as well as this farm estate?"

The squire shook his jowls like a wary bulldog, peering at Harry over his plate. "Never you mind my interests on this estate."

"Da," Miss Gannett warned. "It's only natural Lord Harry will want to know such things for the marriage settlements."

And there was the rocky shoal in this deep sea.

Harry lost his appetite. Not so the squire, who speared a piece of roast beef into his mouth and considered Harry narrowly as he chewed.

"It's a pretty property," he finally allowed. "Some fourteen hundred hectares divided evenly between arable and pasturage. And I've another farm up by Truro of some six hundred hectares."

"And the Hall," Miss Gannett added. "Our family has been on this land since the days of the Conqueror."

Harry tried to give all this information the proper interest, but he was a navy man and knew halyards, not hectares. "Impressive," was all he could manage.

The word seemed to please the squire—he sat back in his chair and took a deep drink of his dinner wine. "And you? What have you to show for yourself?"

"Not much, I am afraid, sir," Harry was happy to lie. "After twelve years of service to His Majesty's Royal Navy I find myself injured and without a career, put ashore to fend for myself." Which he had done superbly, even if he did say so himself, earning the rank of Post Captain at a young age and winning a more than respectable fortune for himself in prize monies from ships he and his men had captured. But the squire didn't need to know that.

"And your father, the marquess? Could he not be expected to do something for you?"

"He did so by buying my place aboard ship twelve years ago. His estate is entirely entailed upon my brother, the Viscount Redgrave."

Though it was his own particular kind of hell to paint himself as some sort of idle ne'er-do-well, Harry attempted to do so. "Damn fine claret, sir." He toasted the squire and drained his goblet, holding it up for immediate refilling.

The squire said nothing, but when Harry's glass had been filled, he indicated to the servants to take the decanter of wine away. "Can't respect a man who don't work. And can't hold his liquor."

Excellent. Harry lobbed another shot across the squire's bow. "This seems a snug enough berth." He cast a glad eye about the hall. "Though I don't take up much room."

"Devil take you for a greedy pup." The squire thumped his fist upon the table, making the cutlery jump, but his descent into a tirade was stopped by the arrival of his steward.

"Message, Squire, from the vicar."

Harry's hand tightened into a fist—the enemy was within his sights.

The squire opened the note, read it, and then tossed it directly into the low fire. "You'll excuse me." He scraped back his chair. "Elly. Captain Beck." He went immediately out, leaving Harry no excuse to follow.

Elowen Gannett carried on eating her dinner as if nothing had happened. Indeed, there was a small, satisfied smile across her lips, as if the idea of dining alone with Harry was quite to her tastes. "Do tell me more about yourself, Captain Lord Harry."

Harry had much rather talk of what business with the vicar might take the squire from his keenly anticipated dinner. "There is not much to tell, Miss Gannett. But—"

"Do you like me?"

The blunt question took Harry off guard, but he was equal to the moment. "I hardly know you, Miss Gannett."

She waved away his concern. "That hardly signifies. We will have ample time to get to know each other once we are married."

"Miss Gannett." Harry tried to make his voice gentle, to soften the blow. "I have told your father that I am not free to marry without my father's consent."

But Elly Gannett was made of sterner stuff and weathered his blow with ease. "A second son with no career marrying the heiress to a very pretty property? I should think your father will agree quick enough." She smiled at him, as if such news ought to encourage him. "And besides, what matters his approval if he can do nothing for you anyway? The important thing is that *I* can do something for you. And you can do something for me."

It was as if a chill wind had blown straight down his spine. Kent's warning came back to him—*watch your back*. "And what is that?"

"You are an experienced sea captain, are you not?"

"Aye." That truth was easy enough to give.

"Then tell me what you see." She got up from the table before Harry could hold her chair and led him to the back of the house, where a lawn overlooked the sea. "Look down there. What do you see?"

What Harry saw sent that cold sense of purpose sliding

under his skin like a blade. "A perfectly sheltered landing place."

"Just so." She rewarded his acuity with a knowing smile. "What you can't see, but which I am sure you can guess at, are the caves for smuggling—the free trade, as we call it." She waited, gauging his reaction, but when he betrayed neither surprise nor outrage, she went on. "I'm not supposed to know anything about it, but, of course I do—I have eyes and ears, and I know French claret when it is served at my father's table. And I can see my father abandoning his good dinner to follow some sudden instruction to move a cargo into the caves or from the caves into the countryside. Everything at the last moment." She turned to him. "With proper management, the tuns of wine and brandy that might be put into our caves tonight would be opened and served in the public houses of Taunton and Bristol tomorrow. But there is no proper management. There is only my father jumping to do someone else's bidding. And stacks of useless grain and flour that cannot be sold for a profit, and attracts foul rats." She gave her curls a vehement shake. "Which is where you, my dear captain, come in."

Harry could not quite follow all of her logic. "For my experience with rats?"

"Perhaps. I can manage things on the land—I need you to manage things asea. Someday soon—when my da dies, or can no longer command the villagers to his bidding—I want *my* chance. But I can have it sooner if I have a husband who understands time and tides and can convince Da to do as I suggest."

"Why do you simply not suggest it now, yourself."

She made a female sound of disdain. "I have. I have told him that the entire operation needs to be run more like a shipping firm and less like a hotchpotch of farmers and fishermen. But he doesn't listen. He doesn't think I have a thought in my head. No one does—the more fools them."

Harry was one of those fools—he had been so entirely taken in by her wide, innocent eyes and breathless appearance, that he hadn't seen her shrewd ambition.

Another thought intruded. "Was it really even your apple, at the fête?"

"What do you think?" But her smile was answer enough. "Suffice it to say, I picked *you*, Lord Harry. Because I need you to get rid of another who fancies himself my father's son-in-law. I don't think he's the right man for the job. Or for me." She turned those lethal golden eyes on Harry. "I think you are."

Harry knew he was—but for an entirely different reason than ambitious Miss Elowen Gannett had in mind. Because he was entirely ambitious, too.

He gave her his brightest smile. "My dear Elly, tell me about this useless grain."

CHAPTER 13

"NESSA?" TRESSA BURST into their shared bedchamber well after one o'clock in the afternoon. "Nessa, he's here."

There was only one person Nessa could imagine as he—she had cried herself to sleep over him. But she also had not seen her sister all morning—when Nessa had awoken before dawn, Tressa's side of the bed had been empty and cold. "Where have you been?"

"Not now." Tressa dismissed her absence with an impatient wave. "Lord Harry is here. He's come for you."

"Come for me?" She had left him yesterday to escape his questions about the trade and had been taxing herself with how on earth she was to seek him out to do as her father bade.

Tressa had none of her sister's trepidation. "Come to call upon you! I heard him in at the door—Miss Teague, he asked for. But Papa has taken him into his book room and closed the door. It can only mean one thing!"

Nessa was not nearly so sanguine. "It can mean many things." Harry was not above subterfuge and might have called to see her father, who had also been absent at breakfast—like Tressa's bed, her father's book room had been cold and empty.

"Hadn't you better go down and find out?"

Nessa pushed aside the unease that sat like cold porridge in her belly and ventured down the creaking stairs to find the door to the book room closed. But if Harry was not above subterfuge, neither was she. She put her ear to the door.

"So, Lord Harry." There was a pause where her father seemed to be settling himself behind his desk. "What brings you to our door after all these years?"

"It has been a long time since I was last here, hasn't it?"

"Indeed. But you've been in Bocka Morrow some days now, for I understand you're staying up at Castle Keyvnor?"

If Harry had not understood that there was little privacy in a village, he knew it now. "Yes, Reverend Teague. And I did speak to your daughter at the Allantide fête."

"Nessa. Yes." Her father paused as if gathering his thoughts. "Did you enjoy your sail the other day?"

To his credit—or to his experience with facing calmly irate fathers—Harry answered straightaway. "Yes, sir. My injury makes prolonged exercise difficult, but as a navy man I much prefer being out of doors. So, the dory was a marvelous respite. I do so miss the sea."

Nessa shifted to try and hear better, but the door creaked loudly under her weight.

"Come," her father called. "Ah, Nessa. There you are," he said in the same tone of mild surprise he used every time he saw her.

Harry stood at her entrance. "Good morning, Miss Teague."

All her awkwardness returned at the mere sight of his

overwhelming handsomeness—Nessa made a graceless curtsey. "Good morning, Captain Beck."

He rewarded her with a quick flash of a smile. "I had come to ask if I might borrow your sailing dory this afternoon. You were kind enough to indulge an invalid navy man yesterday, but I dare not trespass upon your time again today."

"Oh, Nessa will be happy to take you out," he father answered. "She has nothing better to do."

This was her father making sure that she had not forgot what she was supposed to do—keep Harry "out of the way". Still, her father's assertion that she had nothing better to do rankled. As did the question of why he wanted Harry out of the way.

"There is some very interesting scenery to the south, very good sailing, that will interest Lord Harry." Her father was already waving them off and turning back to his books. Already dismissing Nessa from his mind. "There's a good girl."

Well then. "I'll just get my cloak."

Harry followed her out into the corridor and touched her elbow, as if he were about to speak, when Cods the ill-timed curate clomped into the passage. After their last exchange, Nessa was still in no mood for pleasantries. Apparently, neither was Cods—he ignored her.

"Good morning, Lord Henry. We have not been properly introduced"—this was accompanied by a shifting glance at her—"but I am James Coddington, curate of the parish."

Despite the breach of civility in introducing himself to a man of superior rank and standing, Cods was met with a polite and immediate bow from Harry. "Mr. Coddington. Good morning."

"It's Captain Beck, actually, Mr. Coddington," Nessa

corrected, if for no other reason than she was tired of being ignored or taken for granted.

Cods continued to ignore her, focusing all his condescension on Harry. "It must have been you I happened to see as I made my way from an ailing parishioner's cottage on the Gannett farmstead last night, my lord. I hope you had a pleasant dinner there?"

If Nessa had not realized Cods had a cruel streak, she knew it now by the blistering ache that blossomed in her chest—she had so conveniently forgotten Elowen Gannett and her claim on Harry. Harry's kisses had made her forget.

"Indeed, sir." Harry had none of her embarrassment. "Very pleasant. I hope your work for the parish does not often take you away from the church and manse at inhospitable hours?"

"I go where I am bid upon the Lord's work," Cods said, eager to impress his piety upon a potential patron—perhaps he had his eye upon a living in the Marquess of Halesworth's gift.

"How very dedicated."

Cods barely managed not to preen. "One does one's best."

"Indeed." Harry politely returned his attention to Nessa. "Shall we, Miss Teague?"

There was nothing for it but to allow Harry to take her elbow and steer her not down through the village toward the quay, but in the opposite direction—out through the manse's orchard and into the wood beyond.

As soon as they were well beyond sight of the house, he came characteristically straight to his point. "First, I should like to first apologize to you. For yesterday. For taking liberties that were not mine to take."

She was tired of ploys and stratagems and unspoken half-truths. "They may not have been yours to take, Harry, but they were mine to give."

"Because your father asked you to?"

"No." She spoke before she could think better of it. Before her father's will could impose itself upon her one heart's desire. "I went sailing with you yesterday because I wanted to. For myself, alone."

He was still wary. "And now?"

Heat and fear built up like hot, unshed tears in her throat. "I don't know." She gave him the uncomfortable truth. "I can't tell if you want to be with me because you like me or if you're trying to find out more about the trade."

"Nessa." He drew close and took hold of her arms. So close she had to tilt her head up to look at him. So close he might have kissed her, right there in the dappled orchard.

Except that he didn't.

"Nessa." He touched the side of her face. "I need to tell you the truth."

She liked him all the more for respecting her enough to tell her the truth—unlike everyone else around her. Even if it made her stomach knot up into a hot, miserable ball.

"I had thought I could do this without involving you." He shook his head as his voice trailed away. "But I saw your face when your father bid you accompany me. I could see the hurt in your eyes. The betrayal."

Nessa felt as if her whole body, every piece of skin, every muscle and sinew and organ went still. "No." She had to make him understand. "It was not you, but the task—he asked me to keep you out of the way, away from the free trade."

"He suspects me—with good reason." Harry held her upper arms, steadying her, as if for a blow. "The truth is, I have been tasked by the Admiralty with investigating the free traders, and finding out exactly who is involved—"

"Harry, everyone is." Surely, he knew this. Surely by now,

he understood. "The whole village—everyone takes shares in the cargoes."

The hard look in his eyes stopped her breath. "Does everyone take a share in treason?"

Her hands went cold with shock. "No." She tried to pull her hands away.

He held on. "More than just French brandy, lace and wine come into Bocka Morrow's caves, Nessa. Someone in this village has been sending and receiving information and more from the French. Treating with the enemy. And I think that someone is your father."

"No." Her knees knocked hard together as if the ground had shifted under her feet. She felt upended and wrong, as if the world could not possibly right itself. "Why would you think that?"

But Nessa was already casting her mind back through the years, when the whole Teague family, including her mother and sisters, and the boys from the school, had all played their part and helped move cargoes as a way to augment her father's small income from the church living and the school. She was already remembering the reasoning her father had employed to justify breaking the law—it had always been that way. She tallied the effort they had spent expanding the cellars beneath the manse so they might store more of the cargo.

She saw through fresh eyes each and every transgression.

She had turned her eyes from it—she had insulated herself with her wild imaginings and fairy tale-like hopes that Lord Harry Beck would come back and sweep her off her feet and take her away from it all.

And he had come back, only now he was going to sweep the village clean.

"He sent word to Squire Gannett, last night, Nessa. And

he wanted you to take me south today, away from whatever is supposed to be going on."

Nessa pushed aside the thin blade of jealousy that slid under her skin at the mere mention of the Gannett name. She turned a deaf ear to the reminder that as far as the village was concerned, Elowen Gannett and Harry were betrothed. And she completely ignored the fact that she had no idea where either her father or her sister had been last night. "He often goes out into the parish, when he is called."

"Does he? Or does he go to move sacks of grain and flour in the Gannett's caves? Grain imported from France. Enough to supply several bakeries."

"How has that anything to do with my father?" Nessa did not understand. "And the cost of bread is cheaper here than in France." She still read the newspapers, even if she wasn't searching for mention of Harry.

"Exactly. And the sacks were old—they had been piling up there for months."

"But what has it to do with my father?"

"I asked myself the same questions. Elowen Gannett didn't know why the flour was being stored in her cave either. But she knew it had been put there, unloaded not by her father's usual crew, but by boys from your father's school."

The realization was like a hard slap to her face—full of burning, painful shame and confusion. She didn't want to see the truth of Harry's assumptions or acknowledge that it might be possible—her father, the Reverend Teague, the Vicar of Saint David's Church and pillar of local society, might be a traitor.

CHAPTER 14

"MY LORD HARRY?"

At the edge of the wood, where pasture gave way to the trees, a groom in his father's livery stood squinting into the shade of the forest. "Message for you, my lord, from Castle Keyvnor."

"How the devil did he find me?" Especially when he had been at such great pains not to be found. Devil take it, he was in the middle of a goddamned wood. Trying to tell the woman he loved that her father was likely a traitor.

What had Nessa said? There's precious little privacy in a small village.

Harry tore open his father's seal before he had time to prepare himself to be astonished. The news knocked the wind from his sails—and the breath from his lungs. "My sister is getting married. This day." He read it again to make sure he had not imagined it. "My sister, Charlotte, is marrying Adam Vail." His sister, with whom he ought to have been spending his time, was getting married this very morning to the heir of Viscount Lynwood, another man

Harry suspected was tied into the knotted skein of treason with the vicar.

An alarm only less livid than rage lit in his chest. Devil take Vail if the man were mixing his sister up in all this.

"I must return immediately to Castle Keyvnor." A lifetime of obedience to duty had Harry making his excuses to Nessa. "I must go to my sister. But…" There was too much left unsaid. Too much he wanted and needed to discuss. "This is deadly serious, Nessa. Neither I nor the Admiralty can turn a blind eye to treason. We must put a stop to it. The fate of our country depends upon our actions."

Nessa closed her eyes, as if the prospect of her father being the traitor caused her physical pain. But she was no coward, Nessa Teague. "What am I to do?" she asked finally.

The surge of elation flooding his best was relief. He exercised it by pressing a kiss to her hand. "Just watch him. Watch what he does, where he goes and who he meets. Watch him for me."

"Harry. He's my father."

She was steadfast and loyal—two of the reasons he loved her. "Then watch him to prove me wrong."

The idea seemed to steady her—color came back to her face. "Aye?"

"Aye. Prove me wrong, Nessa. And I'll thank you for it all the rest of my days."

And he kissed her to prove it. He kissed her with all the force and heat of his want and his surety and his understanding of the burden he was placing upon her. He kissed her because he loved her and he wanted more than anything to be wrong.

Even if he knew to his bones that he wasn't.

The knowledge was enough to drive a man to drink. "Come." He called to the servant. "Take me to Castle Keyvnor by way of the Crown & Anchor."

THE MOMENT NESSA closed the door to her bedchamber late that afternoon, Tressa was at her. "What did he want?"

Nessa tried to keep from wearing her knowledge and fear on her face, but she was no card player. And Tressa knew her too well. But before she would satisfy her sister's rampant curiosity, Nessa had a question of her own. "Where were you last night?"

"Where were you just now?"

"With Lord Harry. And then walking." Trying to outpace her restless unhappiness. Trying to think. To choose between the Devil and the deep blue sea. "And you?"

Tressa wiped her hand down the side of her skirt, leaving a surprisingly damp smudge. "I was at Black Cove," she admitted. "I was with someone—someone I think is a friend to Lord Harry."

"Someone from the Admiralty?"

"I think so."

"And are *you* a friend to this man?"

"Are you a friend to Lord Harry?"

They might go about in circles in this manner all night. But Nessa knew her sister almost as well as she knew herself. Tressa was many things—brash, unhappy and dissatisfied with the small life their village afforded her—but she knew wrong from right. She was not a traitor.

At least Nessa prayed so. "Harry said they think it's treason, Tressa."

Tressa let out the shaky breath she seemed to have been holding. "I think they think it's Papa." Her voice broke. "What if it is?"

To hear her own fears spoken aloud was like a death knell from the church belfry. "What if it isn't?"

"Papa was there last night, Nessa. In the cave at Black Cove. Talking to the old viscount."

"That doesn't mean he was talking treason." But if it was their father trading secrets with the French, did they have a moral obligation to help Harry and the Admiralty bring him to justice and possibly see him hanged? Or did they have a greater obligation to their family to try and prove Harry wrong?

Nessa rested her weary head on her hand and stared out the window at the lengthening afternoon shadows. Harry's sister—who did not apparently need an apple or a charm to find love or get a husband—was probably married by now and the castle would be alight with festivities. Festivities to which Nessa would never be invited. Never could be, were her father proved to be a traitor.

Tressa laid her head on Nessa's shoulder. "What are we going to do?"

Harry had asked her to watch. Below in the churchyard, she watched Cods the Curate return from another one of his endless walks. And then she watched her father come out to speak to him. They were too far away for Nessa to make out any actual words—all she could hear were the hissing sounds of furious whispering, tense and full of recrimination.

She leaned as far out on the sill as she dared, listening to the low, insistent voices.

"You'll do as you're told."

Nessa could not tell who had spoken, but Cods was the one leaving, stalking off toward the vestry, while her father stood alone by the garden gate in the falling light.

"I'm going down," she decided, though she ached with the thought of what might come of it. "I'm going to confront him."

"Nessa." The urgency of Tressa's whisper stopped her. "I think Cods is climbing the belfry. I can see his lamp."

Nessa turned back to watch as Cods, indeed, climbed onto the open parapet atop the belfry, though there was no reason for him to do so—it was too early for the call to evensong. And he did not go to the bells, but raised his shuttered lantern high, opening the louvers three times, in three bright measured flashes, sending his signal out toward the sea.

"Did you see that?" Tressa clutched at Nessa's hand.

"I did." She saw more than just the flashes of light—she saw the evidence that Harry had given her and that she had figured out for herself, in a new light.

"What are you going to do?"

Nessa's pulse began to pound in her ears. There was only one thing to do. "Follow him." Watch *him*. Prove to Harry that it was *not* her father who was the traitor.

"I'm coming with you," Tressa vowed.

"No. You need to warn your friend from the Admiralty."

"Captain Kent."

"Aye. I'll get word to Harry up at Castle Keyvnor."

Tressa gripped her fingers tight and left. Nessa went down the back stairs to her father's book room.

"Ah, Nessa." her father was coming out. "Pray tell your mama, that I will be out for some while. There's a good girl."

Nessa was done being a good girl. She damned her nerves and planted herself in the middle of the passage. "Where are you going?"

"There are things—" He faltered, uncomfortable with her confrontation. "I have business—"

"Business with the free traders?"

Her father, at last, met her eyes. "This is different. This is wrong. I didn't see that before. None of us did. We didn't see the harm." He paused and took a deep breath. "But we've had enough, the squire and I. We've got to stop him."

His words washed over Nessa like a benediction. He might not be the most passionate of fathers, or the most disciplined of schoolmasters, or the most diligent of clergymen. But he was a good man. Weak he might be, but a traitor he was not—of this she was sure.

"I have betrayed my faith and my convictions as a clergyman." He was shaking his head as if he were still trying to fathom it out. "I have allowed myself to be led astray."

"By whom?"

"It's all my fault. I never should have brought him here. I should have vetted him properly and found out that he's not even ordained—"

Cods, not her father.

It was Cods who went everywhere, at all hours, with no one the wiser—he had been up on the cliff road above Black Cove when the lugger had come in and he had been out at the Gannett Farmstead last night. Cods who always seemed busy, but never did a lick of work. "It's Cods."

Her father nodded wearily. "I fear he's made the whole of the village his unwitting accomplices."

Cods with his whispers and cautions in people's ears was the traitor. But if there were no privacy in the village, then there were no real secrets, either. "Then get the whole of the village, as well as the squire, to stop him."

Because at that moment, she could see Cods come out of the vestry and turn up the lane. Heading in direction of Castle Keyvnor.

Nessa wasted no time second-guessing herself. "You get the squire," she told her father.

She had made her choice—she had to warn Harry.

CHAPTER 15

*H*ARRY HAD A vertiginous feeling of playing catch up. His younger sister had, in the space of five days, fallen in love and gotten herself married—and here he thought he had been going too fast with Nessa.

The reason given for the bride and groom's nearly unseemly haste to the wedding was astonishing as well—"homicidal ghost" struck him as particularly far-fetched, though Harry himself had lived through too many close calls when nothing but sheer luck would seem to have preserved him to dismiss all assertions of otherworldliness. But it was his opinion that if there were malignant spirits at Castle Keyvnor, they more likely belonged to the living than the dead. Or to the ancient plumbing.

Whether the living were suspicious of the plumbing or not, the marriage was celebrated not in Castle Keyvnor's ancient chapel, but in a Romany encampment on the edge of Banfield lands. It was as strange and irregular as anything Harry had ever seen—and he had been to the end of the world and back.

There was another strange and irregular thing—the

absence of the groom's grandfather, Viscount Lynwood. Adam Vail was Lynwood's heir and the future owner of Hollybrook Park. And Black Cove. Which made the absence of his *paterfamilias* notable. And problematic. And deeply, deeply curious.

As soon as the irregular celebration that made his sister the happiest of women—and his father one of the most relieved of men—reached its dancing, drinking zenith, Harry slipped away from the merrymaking and made his solitary way across the park onto Hollybrook land.

The house above the cliffs lay quiet—most of the staff were presumably helping with the wedding celebrations—but a few lamps burned inside.

Harry made a circuit of the house in the falling twilight, assessing its structure and position in the rocky landscape, in the same manner that he would have read an enemy's strength at sea. There were no guns bristling from the windows of Hollybrook, but Harry noted the movement of light spilling through the windows onto the lawns to the library. Within, an older man—presumably the Viscount Lynwood—emerged from a door hidden in the paneling next to the chimney-piece, alone and muttering, carrying a lamp in one hand and cradling dusty bottle of brandy in the other.

The viscount was both deeply out of breath and in his cups—he spilled more illicit French brandy on the rug than into his glass. But what he did manage to pour was more than sufficient to drown his sorrows—the bottle soon fell to the floor and the old man fell to snoring into his cravat.

Harry entered through an open library window. Though stealth had never been one of his better qualities—it was an entirely useless skill aboard ship where men were quartered cheek by jowl—the viscount was too cup-shot to notice. Harry simply picked up the lamp from where it had been dropped and slipped down the darkened stairwell.

The first few flights of stairs, descending through the servants' and cellar levels of the house, were made of wood, but soon thereafter they turned to stone, hewn out of the rock. Harry checked the compass on the head of his cane, and found it pointed southwest, toward the sea.

The steps grew narrower and steeper, until Harry lost count of the steps, and the air grew stale and musty. But the sure and steady pulse of purpose drummed through his veins, lending him enough strength that his leg very nearly ceased to pain him.

At last, a fresh breeze of salty air wafted up the tight staircase and he finally came out into a high, naturally vaulted cavern. A dry rock floor sloped down to sand nearer to the cave's entrance to the southwest. Harry checked his timepiece—the tide was on the ebb and the cave's entrance below the high tide line would not be passable for nearly another hour.

He began his inspection of the rows of neatly stacked barrels of French brandy and larger casks of wine stored well above the waterline, row upon row. There was nothing out of the ordinary—no flour or grain.

Harry contemplated a tun of *vin ordinaire*, wondering what he had missed, when he felt a cooler draft of air that raised the hair on the nape of his neck.

If he were another man, he might have blamed the eerie chill on the ghost of Black Cove, but his well-honed sense of logic urged him to wet his thumb and follow the thin thread of moving air to an angled fissure that concealed a narrow, gated passage. The rusted iron gate was closed, but not locked, and the long passage sloped slowly upward—and according to his compass, back toward the south. Back toward Castle Keyvnor.

Harry raised the lantern, considering, but already his feet were moving, as if an unseen ghost was pushing him, guiding him onward. He followed the tunnel four cable lengths through the rock, until it finally opened into a low-ceilinged storage room packed tightly with an odd assortment of old casks, kegs, and crates.

Harry's already chilled hackles rose instantly, for there was a particular sort of familiarity to the goods that made his blood run cold—he had overseen the lading, un-crating and stowage of similar casks and boxes upon his own ships. There was a stack of half-casks thick with dust and the words "Loire et Cher" stenciled on their lids, while another batch, less thickly covered, were imprinted with "Yonne"—French-mined amber flints of various sizes for muskets, pistols and cannon.

On the other side of the cavern, barrels marked "Essonne" for the mill outside Paris— standard hundred-pound kegs of black powder. And all along one wall were crates about five feet long, stacked five deep, and marked "Charleville-Mézières"—French 1777 model muskets from the armory in the Ardennes. Guns he had faced standing on the quarter-deck of his ship, the target of sharp-eyed enemy shooters stationed in the mast tops.

All covered in dust, with the exception of three crates set at a right angle to the others, marked "Maubeuge" after the arsenal in northern France that was closest to the Channel and transport to Cornwall.

Harry wielded his cane like an oaken handspike and pried open the corner of one of the long crates to prove to himself that he was right. And there they were, just as he had anticipated—French flintlock muskets, nestled in straw and packed two dozen to a case. With eight stacks, two deep and ten crates high, there were nearly four thousand guns gathering dust within the dark. Enough guns for a bloody army.

Harry's eye went back to the lettering marking the open crate—Maubeuge, the armory closest to the port of

Boulogne, where Napoleon had some years earlier gathered his Army of the Ocean Coasts. The original plan to cross the Channel and invade England had been abandoned over ten years ago—the forces gathered at Boulogne dispersed across France into the *Grande Armée*.

Understanding hit Harry harder than French chain shot ever had—the plan clearly hadn't been abandoned. It had simply been changed. In this cave far beneath Castle Keyvnor, Harry was standing amidst the munitions that would supply an invasion of the island fortress of England.

NESSA HURRIED THROUGH the churchyard in time to see Cods sweep through the lichgate and through the village at such a clip that even long-legged Nessa had to run to keep up. She kept to the edges of the lane, hugging the lengthening shadows, rapidly trying to formulate a plan—she would follow Cods to the castle, and then enter through the kitchens where she could send for Harry, and tell him of her suspicions.

But before he reached the bridge that led across the dry moat to Keyvnor's portcullis, Cods veered off into a stretch of parkland that sloped away from the foot of the castle cliffs, a dark figure merging into the green and black background.

Nessa halted on the edge of the path, debating whether she should follow Cods or continue to the castle to find Harry. But the castle was dark and silent—clearly no wedding celebration was taking place there. Perhaps the wedding was held at Hollybrook Park—the direction that Cods was now heading.

She felt propelled after him, as if the roaming ghosts of Castle Keyvnor were urging her on. So, she tore after him, until a light flared like a beacon in the near distance—Cod's lantern illuminating the velvet night to reveal the mossy headstones of the Banfield family graveyard.

For a moment, doubt washed over Nessa like a cold rain —perhaps she and the ghosts were wrong. Perhaps the curate had come all this way just to pray. But what she heard was not prayers, but the rattle of keys and the metallic shriek of the rusty gate of the mausoleum being opened. And then the light from the lantern winked out, seemingly to be swallowed whole by the cliffside.

Cods had disappeared beneath the mausoleum.

Nessa crept closer still, listening intently and staring into the dark—there was no sound, no light. She ventured closer until she could smell the cool and damp of the mausoleum air—it smelt of death and decay and…salt. The fresh salt air from the sea below the cliffs.

There had always been stories, half-forgotten rumors that the whole of the coast was riddled with hidden passages and connected by underground tunnels—there was even a rumor that a passage led directly from the low tide mark at the harbor straight into the cellar of the Crown & Anchor public house.

Castle Keyvnor had always stood apart from those stories —it had been well known in the village that the old Earl Banfield disapproved of the trade and took no part in it. But neither had he interfered. And his castle had stood upon the cliffs above Bocka Morrow for centuries—the medieval fortress could harbor secret, ancient passages even if the current titleholder had no use for them.

As proof, the lock on the gate, now that Nessa got close enough to inspect it in the falling dark, was new. And it seemed Cods, the parish curate, and not the heir of the Earl of Banfield, had the keys.

Fortunately for Nessa the bars were old and wide. And she, who had always been judged too tall and too gawky, was just lathy enough to squeeze herself through and into the mausoleum.

What she thought she might do, with no light and no way of stopping Cods, Nessa did not know. But she had come too far to stop and she could follow the sound of Cod's leather-soled shoes slapping rhythmically against the stone steps as the stairway led her down, down into the dark earth.

The air grew saltier, and then cold, and colder still. In the endless dark, Nessa started to see bits of blue and red at the corners of her vision, as if the ghosts rumored to inhabit the castle had decided to accompany her along. A cold blast of air chilled the back of her neck and alarm raised goosebumps all down her spine, but it was as if the spirit of the place were urging her onward, compelling her to act as a witness. To find out exactly where Cods had gone, and who he had gone to meet before she turned back to report her findings.

But it was one thing to be determined—to know what was right—and another thing entirely to find the courage to push on through the dark. But perhaps, she had more determination than she knew. Perhaps, it had been determination that had kept her dreaming through each boring day before Harry had come back that had kept her copying sermons without giving into despair. Because she kept onward, down the steep stair until, finally, a slight glow of light beckoned.

Nessa slowed and made the last few steps with the utmost caution, pressing close to the wall, listening carefully for any sound that might indicate where Cods had gone.

There was nothing but the distant lapping of water against rock. Nothing but a sudden, silent rush of movement, before a hand wrapped itself around her mouth, smothering the life from her.

CHAPTER 16

"NESSA? DAMN YOUR eyes." Harry recognized her by the subtle scent of primrose, and the long lithe line of her body pressed tight against his. He instantly released his hand from her mouth but didn't let go. "Tell me you're not up to your pretty neck in this business."

"Only to my ankles. I followed Cods," Nessa told him in an urgent whisper.

Her father's henchman. Harry had let him slip past.

"*He's* the one," she insisted. "He's the one in charge, making my father and everyone from the fisherfolk to Squire Gannett do his bidding. He signaled to someone offshore from the belfry but we couldn't see if anyone answered. That's why I followed him—to see who he meets."

"We?"

"Tressa and I. I sent her for your friend—Captain Kent."

"Excellent." Harry breathed a trifle easier—Kent knew his suspicions and would have put to sea immediately to track whatever ship—or ships—were approaching. Devil take them if there were more than one ship.

And damn them all to hell if it were the invasion.

Harry had to do everything in his power to stop them and he had to do it now. He had to destroy the munitions before Coddington and the French could reach them.

But the gunpowder would turn the whole of the cavern into a bomb that would blow out every passage, snuffing out the air, and likely igniting a secondary explosion of the flammable brandy.

Every instinct in his body, every ounce of his experience at war, told him there would be no escape. "Go back now." He pushed her toward the stair. "Go as fast as you can to the top and get clear of the entrance." He would wait as long as he could—

"It's locked at the top—you couldn't get out." She wasn't budging. "But why? What are you planning to do?"

"The place is full to the rafters with munitions—materiel for Napoleon's army to use when they invade England. I'm going to blow it all up."

"But how are you going to get out?" she demanded. "The staircase will act like a chimney."

"I'm certain it connects to Black Cove," he assured her. It would be a close run thing no matter how he did it, to outrun the explosion with his leg. But he knew his duty and the ramifications of his decisions better than most men—he knew what it was to have the fate of men in his hands, including his own.

He would do what needed to be done, no matter the cost.

"No." She was newly adamant, all trace of hesitation and awkward, stammering shyness gone. "I won't leave you to do it alone. I'll light the fire after you've already started for the mouth of the cave. It will be a long run to Black Cove and I'm faster."

She always had been. This was the girl he had known, the girl who had raced him across the shifting sands. And won.

Her logic was as unassailable as her surety. God, he loved her.

"Bring me a keg of that powder." He un-shuttered the lantern and pointed the beam at the kegs of gunpowder. "Carefully, while I—"

But she was already streaking across the cave to do his bidding.

Harry shoved the opened gun crate closer to the larger stack, and then broke open a second crate with his cane, gathered up the straw and piled it loosely like tinder. When Nessa returned with the cask, he flung it hard against the floor to bash it open and spread the black powder along the floor to help the flames find their way to the rest of the casks, giving them less time to escape, but assuring the cache's destruction.

Nessa had already taken up the lantern, all capable understanding. "I'll light the straw first and make sure it catches, then I'll come straight away."

"Aye." He wanted to give her some further instruction, to provide some greater caution. To prolong the moment as long as possible. But there was nothing left to do and only the briefest of instruction left to say. "Mind your skirts."

"I will," she assured him with quiet confidence. "I know what to do."

"Count to twenty and then light it." And then he took her face in his hands and kissed her.

HARRY KISSED HER with a hunger that took the breath from her. He kissed her hard, with force and need and that fierce tenderness, as if he wanted to press his will upon her but knew better.

And then he was gone, moving unevenly for the passage.

Nessa opened the lantern's shutters and trained the wide beam on the dark tunnel to light his way. Twenty, nineteen, eighteen.

She took a moment to tie up her skirts and petticoats as best she could. Fifteen, fourteen.

She shifted the lantern slightly, tracing the path, making sure the way was clear. Ten.

Her heart was beating in her ears. Nine. Her breath was beginning to pump in and out of her chest. Eight.

She had to take the candle out of the lantern and then put it back before she ran or she wouldn't be able to see where she was going. Six. The wax spilled on her shaking fingers. Five. Her other hand gripped the lantern ring convulsively. Four.

She crouched down next to the pile and lowered the candle flame.

Three, two, one.

The first tongue of flame curled sweetly into the straw and then began to lick the wood of the crates. Nessa shoved the candle back into place, burning her fingertips. The candle stub slotted into its well on the second try and she slammed the glass shut and ran for all she was worth.

Her shoes were slick on the stone floor and she skidded, scraping against the wall as she careered into the passage. She ran so fast she felt as if she would outrun the spill of light from the lantern. She ran so hard her steps echoed down the tunnel so loudly she didn't hear Harry until she was upon him.

"Go!" he shouted and pushed her in front of him, as if he could somehow shield her with his body. "Go."

She needed no further encouragement but clutched his hand in hers and put her head down to race for the end of the passage, for once thankful of her long legs that ate up the yards.

Behind them, she heard the fire beginning to roar and smelled the smoke billowing down the passage after them. On they ran, with their eyes watering, their lungs burning, and their legs aching.

They ran until the way to Black Cove was barred by an iron gate.

Nessa slammed her hands against it, rattling the lock. "It's bolted!"

Harry was already beside her, laying his shoulder into it hard. But though it rattled, the lock held. "My stick." He levered his cane into the small gap and worked it furiously, making the bars creak with strain. "If only I could get at it from the other side and work the hinges—"

These bars were newer and tighter than the gate of the mausoleum above, but Nessa squeezed herself between them, sucking in her breath, angling her head and pressing with all her might, until the pain nearly stopped her. Until Harry laid his hand to her shoulder and uncremoniously shoved her through.

"Go," he ordered again.

She didn't even bother to argue. Instead, she pulled his cane through the bars and went for the lock from a different angle.

"There," he encouraged, never looking behind his back where an eerie orange glow was lighting up the passage. Where at any moment the gunpowder was going to explode. "Lever it upwards."

She did so, working frantically with little result, until she saw the hinge lift slightly. She repositioned the cane to better force the gate up and off the top hinge. And then she was jumping out of the way as Harry kicked the gate the rest of the way down.

She barely had time to catch her breath before he had taken her hand in a tight, tenacious grip, pulling her after him, running as fast as their legs would carry them down the rows and rows of barrels and wine tuns, toward the mouth of Black Cave. Everything around them was flammable and more likely to fan the flames of the fire than quench them.

She ran like hell was going to ignite behind her.

Until hell was in front of her—Cods blocked the way, standing on the pier-like scaffolding atop the deep tide pool, brandishing a pistol.

Nessa felt her steps falter and her heart give out.

She was going to die. One way or another. She was going to die before she could ever tell Harry that she loved him, that she had always loved him, and that she was his one and only true love.

She knew it by the rending pain in her chest that was her heart well and truly breaking.

And by the hellish blast of the inferno bearing down upon them.

But Harry was perhaps not so prepared to die. For he never stopped, never slowed. He but wrapped his arms tightly around her and sailed her straight past Cod's gun and plunged them headlong into the dark salt sea.

CHAPTER 17

*H*ARRY TWISTED HIS body, so that as they flew past the slack-jawed Coddington, who raised his pistol and fired—just as Harry knew he would—the ball would hit him instead of Nessa.

But if it did, he didn't feel it.

They plunged into the frigid water and Nessa immediately tried to free her arms, to kick and move to counter the icy chill. But Harry held her fast, dragging her downward like an anchor. Taking her as far out of harm's way as he possibly could.

She broke free of his hold and kicked away, surging for the surface, but he snagged her hair, twisting it around his palm like a rope, and dragged her down backwards.

And not a moment too soon.

The air above flashed orange and white, and the shock of the explosion punched through the water like a cannon shot. The surface convulsed and shifted, and dark bits of rock and God knew what else rained down upon them. A hunk of rock grazed hard against his shoulder, even as Harry pulled them deeper, away from the all-consuming conflagration above.

A sharp shard of rock whizzed toward Nessa, and she understood his urgency then. She turned back toward him and began to kick and stroke alongside him to find the mouth of the cave hidden in the darkness.

Before them, the black wall of the cliff loomed, stretched downward as far as he could see. Heat built like steam in his chest. The water grew darker still as the light above was snuffed out like an extinguished wink.

The utter darkness was momentarily disorienting and Harry cracked his head hard against a rock, blanking his vision and scraping his temple. Fear clawed at him, vicious and unreasonable, shredding the last of his composure.

He should have sent her up the stair. He should have sent her on ahead, instead of letting her light the fire. He should never have involved her in the first place, never revealed himself, because now they might both die, drowned in the gaping maw of the black sea.

It was Nessa's hand that pulled him back, grasping his sleeve to tug him toward a greener shade of black—the spill of moonlight from outside filtering down through the water.

Harry blinked to clear his vision, and pulled hard for it, his lungs burning, his hands clutching Nessa close as they scraped under the lip of rock, and finally, finally started to rise.

They broke the surface like thrashing pilchards, spitting and gasping. Nessa choked on mouthful of water, and her head slipped under.

Harry hauled her into his arms. "I've got you," he promised.

"I'm all right," she gasped, though her lips were shaking, her teeth chattering together from the cold and shock. Her legs kept tangling in her skirts, making it hard for her to keep her head above water.

"You saved me." She was crying as she said it, wrapping her arms around him as if she would never let him go.

Which was fine with him. "Of course I did." Though he nearly drowned them both in the process. "But you saved me, too. In the water. And at the gate." He fought for breath. "You saved us both."

She had been more than right—he did need her. He always had—he always would.

"Marry me, Nessa Teague. Before we both drown."

His words rose like frozen ghosts over the cold water, wreathing them in rime. Which meant that if they did not pull themselves from the water as soon as possible, they still might never pledge their undying—and that was important, the undying part—devotion.

Above them the moon winked down from the dark night sky, illuminating the wall of the cliff rising away into the night. Beneath it, they half-swam, half-floated to shore, bloody and bruised, but essentially unbowed.

The moment his feet touched bottom he gathered her into his arms and carried her as far as the surf line, where she could drag her sodden skirts onto the cold, windswept beach. Harry was right behind her, hauling himself out of the water like a particularly large pilchard.

They lay on the cold shingle for a moment, no more than a foot away from each other, gasping and breathing, and somehow still alive. "I'm sorry I pulled your hair."

Nessa let out a gasping huff of laughter. "Not as sorry as I would have been if you hadn't and had let me be blown to bits." She reached out her hand.

Harry was about to take it, when a shot from across the water echoed wildly off the cliff.

He threw himself on top of her, protecting her body with

his own. And then he was hauling her to her feet and making for the shelter of the boulders edging the shingle.

From the relative safety of the rocks, he saw what he had not before—the outline of the ship that had come to meet Coddington. "A French sloop from the cut of her sail and the rake of her masts," he said.

But he could also see now that the sloop had not been firing at them—its target was the small ship lined across the mouth of Black Cove. "Kent's lugger," he explained. "Captain Matthew Kent of the Royal Navy, though I daresay he wishes he were in a frigate with the fleet at his back."

"I think that is a fleet at his back," Nessa said with some relief. "My father and the squire, I should think, with all the village fisherfolk."

There they were, the faint outlines of a ragtag fleet of luggers and trawlers full of local fishermen lining the horizon and closing off the mouth of the cove. Trapping the sloop within.

For the first time in hours—days even, Harry felt enough relief to take a deep breath and assess the line of battle arrayed before him with professional eyes—the French sloop might have some advantage of firepower, but unless they exercised that advantage immediately, they were as good as lost.

Kent would see that, too—he was no fisherman bungling around in the dark. He was a frigate commander through and through, and before the sloop could bring her guns to bear, Kent was already angling his lugger to aim his long tom guns into her beam.

The concussion from the bow-chasers split the night as the cannon blew a furious hole in the sloop amidships and were immediately hauled back to reload. But there was no need—the French crew had already begun to abandon their ship, diving over the side in the hopes of reaching shore before they were captured.

No chance of that—the luggers swooped into the cove, putting down their ship's boats and scooping up the deserting mariners like pilchards in a pinch net. And something else besides—as the tide receded, the gaping mouth of Black Cave seemed to spit out the long, black-clad form of Coddington's body, floating face down on the silvered surface of the water.

He had done it—they had done it. Harry's work there was well and truly done.

And, in another way, just beginning.

He wrapped his arms around Nessa. "You're freezing." He peeled off his sodden coat and wrapped it around her shoulders. "My poor love."

Her level gaze pierced his in the moonlight. "Am I truly your love?"

"Ah, Nessa. You don't think I would nearly blow you up and drag you underwater just so I could spy on idle pilchard fishermen, do you?"

"Harry." Her smile was all in her blazing blue eyes.

He kissed her with everything he was. Telling her with his mouth and his hands and his body that she was precious to him. That he would protect her. That she was his.

She turned her face up to his and kissed him back. Her touch was light, the barest brush of her lips against his and, for a long moment, he wondered if she wanted nothing more. Then her lips settled more thoroughly upon his, and a jolt of anticipation shuddered down into his chest when she took his bottom lip between hers and tugged gently. And then again, upon his upper lip. And again at the far corner of his mouth, which made him instinctively open to her and kiss her back, moving his lips upon hers with heat and urgency

"Nessa Teague? Nessa Teague!" A voice carried itself down the cliff. "What in the name of all the earth is going on here?"

It was the old witch from the cottage, scrambling down the cliff path. "Come you up here," she ordered. "And let me have a look at you."

They complied, picking their sodden way upward to the cottage slouched against the cliffside like a hunchback crone, their hands clasped tight and their hearts tighter still. There would be a fire, even if it were only dried cow dung, and he could get her out of the raw wind. And back into his arms where she belonged. Now and forever.

CHAPTER 18

"WHAT ON EARTH have you two been up to?" the old woman asked as she herded them into the relative warmth of the cottage. "It felt as if the earth itself moved."

"It should have done." Nessa could barely believe the evening's tally. "We seem to have foiled treason, blown up half of Bocka Morrow, and gotten ourselves burned and drowned and concussed for our trouble."

The widow was nonplussed. "Well done, I'm sure."

The numbness of shock began to wear off enough to admit a sobering pang of regret. "And killed Mr. Coddington." She had wished him ill, but never wished him dead.

"Good riddance," the widow exclaimed. "Waste no remorse on that one, my child. Bad seed, he was. Always trying to get me out of this cottage that the old earl himself vouchsafed to me."

"And why did Banfield do so?" Harry asked.

"Why to keep the trade, and others, out of his caves. Put it about that they were cursed, he did, and I was to sit here above as a caution. Your blowing them up will serve as proof of the curse," she concluded with some satisfaction. "Now, you need to get out of those wet clothes. Both of you."

She shooed them toward the small bedchamber set apart from the rest of the cottage by the fireplace wall, where a wood fire burned cheerfully in the grate. "I've a pot o'mustard for the burns on your back and arms." She followed them with a tray bearing various concoctions. "You'll need to put a thin coating over that mark on his shoulder, Nessa, and this bit of salve on that cut on his forehead. And you're not looking so in the pink, yourself, my dear. You'll both want a good hot toddy to warm your innards." She handed them both steaming mugs. "Get that down quick-like."

"What's in it?" Nessa asked, hoping against hope that the posset wouldn't contain another bitter charm.

Harry had already taken a sip. "A great deal of French brandy, I'd guess."

"'Tis," the old woman confirmed, before she added with a sly wink for Nessa, "and nothing else that won't do you the world of good. Now get you out of those wet clothes to dry before the fire. And you"—she pointed her arthritic finger at Harry—"make sure you warm up your betrothed." And with that, she closed the door behind her.

Harry could have protested that Nessa was not yet his betrothed. He should have protested. But he did not.

And neither did Nessa. Because she wanted it more than anything else in this world.

So she took a deep drink of the posset and hoped that this time, the charm would work. The potent liquid lit up her breath. "Gracious!" At the rate her skin was heating, her underthings would be dry in no time.

Across the room, Harry shucked his sodden shirt over his head, giving her an astonishing view of his spectacular chest. "Gracious," she said again.

Harry laughed. "We'd best leave some of our clothes on or I won't be responsible for what happens."

"I will be," she returned. "Responsible." And she peeled off her wet wool dress to prove it.

"I'd rather you weren't, sweet Nessa. Because we are both under the influence of a great shock, not to mention a great deal of potent brandy, and there are rules about such things. Come sit next to the fire," he urged her, as he opened the pot of mustard.

His matter-of-fact demeanor lessened her shyness, or perhaps it was the toddy that had banished her qualms. Whichever it was, she went to him.

He sat behind her, in front of the fire. "This should help."

His cool fingers touched the round of her shoulder, smearing the paste down her arm. It stung a little going on but seemed to draw the heat out of her skin. Thought it did nothing for the curious tension inside. "I feel all shaky."

"Delayed reaction," he explained. "Which I'm grateful for, because despite being burned and blown up and bumped on the head, I feel rather remarkable." And covering her mouth with his, he showed her just how remarkable.

The tension melted into elation—she felt light and upended, as topsy-turvy as if the waves were tumbling them over and over. Every hint of fatigue vanished. Every weary nerve came alive and tingling.

She wrapped her arms around his neck, pulling him close. So close she could feel the heat from his body. So close she could feel the weave of his woolen coat against the flat of her cheek and the skin above her neckline.

Her breathing began to rise and fall from an entirely different sort of excitement than the fear she had experienced only an hour before. This wasn't exactly fear, but it still felt full of risk. And reward.

The reward was his touch, gentle around her shoulders as he pulled her to him.

They were bound together, inseparable.

The idea filled her with joy that stole her breath and stopped her from speaking. Joy that left a trail of tingling heat and sensation that burrowed beneath her skin and nestled deep into her bones. Joy that tunneled beneath the layers of her stays and shift, and tightened her breasts into needy peaks.

Another shock of heat suffused her face and neck, and spread downward, melting into her, turning her bones liquid and light. Nessa had to put her hand against her stays to assure herself they were still in place—beneath her hand, her pulse battered against her palm.

"Did you mean it, when you asked me to marry you?"

"Aye," he growled against her neck. "And I mean it more than ever, now. Marry me, Nessa Teague. Make me the happiest of men. Tell me you will."

She did not tell him, if only because her heart was too full to speak. She was afraid to believe. Afraid to trust that the magic of the charm had well and truly worked, and she was finally, at long last, getting her heart's desire.

And her body's desire as well, for he had kissed her with such blatant want and need, the near painful ache of longing that had been lodged in her chest moved lower, melting into something warmer and more provocative.

She met his need with her own, slanting her head to take his taut bottom lip between her teeth and bit down gently, delicately, holding him captive to her fresh desire, baiting him with the promise of more. Teasing him into complicit compliance.

But in the next moment she was almost sorry she had teased him so, for she was unprepared for the force of passion she had awakened in him. His hands cupped her chin and he sank into her kiss with abandon, drinking in her lips, pushing her back into the wooden floor.

And she was lost. Lost to everything but the smooth shock of his lips and the comforting rasp of his incipient beard against her skin. Lost to the feel of his thumbs fanning across her cheek, urging her to open to him, and give in to the decadent soft tangle of tongue upon tongue. Lost in the depth of the hungry ache within her, that grew instead of being assuaged.

Hungry for more of the fresh rain taste of him. More of the cedar spice scent of him. More of the careful, decorous feel of him.

She looped her arms around his neck and held him tight, pressing herself into the comforting heat and pliant solidity of his chest, while his tongue touched and caressed hers. All the while, his lips lulled and enticed with growing heat, drugging her with sweet need.

His hands delved into her wet hair, cradling her nape, holding her head at just the right angle, kissing her as if she were a taste he had not known he craved and was still hungry for more.

"Nessa." He said her name the old-fashioned, Cornish way, with a sigh at the beginning and the end. Just the way she liked it. "I love you."

"I love you, too." Nessa whispered the words as loudly as she dared, afraid he would hear and afraid he wouldn't. "I always have." And because the words were never really enough, she turned her hand within his own and raised it to press a kiss to the center of his palm. "And I most assuredly mean to marry you. But first, I have a confession to make."

Harry drew back, and smiled and frowned all at the same time, and she was shot through with that peculiar, familiar ache that was her love for him.

She took a deep, fortifying breath. "You are under the influence of a charm."

"And here I thought it was illegal French brandy."

"I am serious," she insisted, though it was hard to be serious when his hand trailed lazy, sensuous circles upon her shoulder. "It was in the seed cake, the charm, as well as the apple. It was my apple all along, not Elly Gannett's."

"I know." He placed a kiss upon her shoulder. "She confessed to it, the greedy jade."

"Why did you not tell me?"

"Because I was having too much fun getting burned and blown up and falling in cold coves. And falling in love. With you."

"But the charm made you fall in love with me."

"Nessa." His voice was quiet and patient and amused. "You said you had to believe to fall under such a spell."

"Aye." It was the truth.

"And do you believe that you love me?" he asked.

"Aye." She had never believed anything more.

He smiled at her, and it was as if the sun had come up in the middle of the night, blazing in all its glory. "Then I happily submit myself to your spell."

CHAPTER 19

THEY WERE MARRIED properly, in the sight of God, her family and the people of Bocka Morrow on the third Sunday after the banns had been read. Just as they ought—without any unseemly haste.

Harry had no inclination to take her to Suffolk and subject her to his family, so with his leg healed, he did the only sensible thing to do to a tender, newly-wed wife—he took her aboard his ship, the *Lively*. "As I recall, you wanted at least one grand adventure."

"Aye." She took in her new surroundings with wide-eyed enthusiasm. "Indeed, I did. Does this mean that you're going to take me out to sea and out of sight of the land?"

He tucked his head to whisper against the soft skin beneath her ear. "I'm going to take you every single way I can think of before we even get out upon the deep blue sea. But first, I need to take you out of sight of the crew." Harry hustled his bride down the companionway and into his private stern cabin, so he could gather her close enough to kiss that particularly soft spot under her ear. "And although you specified only one adventure, I think it only fair to warn you I am bound and determined to give you an entire lifetime of grand adventures, my Lady Beck. Starting now."

She eyed the hanging bed, suspended from ropes in the ceiling beams. "What kinds of adventures?"

He steered her toward it, discarding her cloak along the way. "The kind that starts with kissing."

"Oh, I like kissing." She reached for his uniform coat. "That is, I like kissing you—I've never kissed anyone else."

He let his sword belt fall to the decking. "And I shall work diligently to keep it that way."

"Oh, I do so like diligence." Her hands were plucking the laces of her bodice. "It's so perfectly charming."

He kissed the corner of her mouth. "I think you're perfectly charming, Nessa Beck."

"I ought to be." She looped her arms around his neck on a sigh. "I paid enough for my charm."

"Did you?" He gathered her close. "And am I worth it?"

"You, my darling Harry, are my one and only true love, and worth every last penny."

THANK YOU FOR READING

Thank you for reading *Between the Devil and the Deep Blue Sea*. I hope you'll take a few minutes out of your day to review this book – your honest opinion is much appreciated. Reviews help introduce readers to new authors they wouldn't otherwise meet.

To keep up to date on Elizabeth's books, sign up for her newsletter and get exclusive excerpts, contests, and more at her WEBSITE.

More from Elizabeth Essex
Please turn the page for an exciting excerpt from Elizabeth Essex's First Reckless Brides novel

ALMOST A SCANDAL,

the story of Matthew's sister Sally Kent, and her adventurous time aboard *HMS Audacious.*

ALMOST A SCANDAL

Portsmouth, England
Autumn 1805

IT WASN'T THE FIRST TIME Sally Kent had donned a worn, hand-me-down uniform from one of her brothers' sea chests, but it was the first time it had felt so completely, perfectly right.

She had always been tall and spare, strong for a girl, but dressed in the uniform of His Majesty's Royal Navy, she felt more than strong. She felt powerful.

Powerful enough to ignore the voice of conscience thundering in her ear, telling her she needed to stay quietly on land and learn to be a young lady. Powerful enough to face down the potential scandal. Powerful enough to abandon her younger brother to his chosen fate.

Because her brother Richard had rejected all claims to duty and honor. He had forsaken his family. He wasn't coming back.

That morning, the very morning he was to have worn his uniform and boarded His Majesty's Ship *Audacious* with all the other candidates for midshipmen, he had disappeared, gone as if he had been swallowed whole by the heavy, obliterating rain.

Richard had left her, quite literally, holding his bag.

And she was going to use it.

Sally closed her mind to the insistent whispering of her conscience, wrapped her breasts in cotton strapping, and put on every single piece of that uniform, from the faded blue midshipman's coat and white breeches, down to the black buckled shoes.

She ignored the uneven pounding of her heart, and took a scissors to her hair. She jammed the dark beaver hat low over her eyes, clattered down the narrow stairs and out of the inn.

She swallowed the sharp edges of her fear, crossed the wet cobbles, and took her brother's place in the rain at the sally port on Portsmouth's rain-drenched quay.

"Richard Kent."

A lieutenant glared at her from under the dripping brim of his cocked hat—an irate lieutenant, his eyes glittering like a flash of black powder.

He stood in the stern of a ship's boat, impervious to the filthy weather and the rise and fall of the vessel tossing fitfully beneath him. The sharp vertical lines of the scowl between his dark brows could have scraped barnacles off a hull, but his low voice was incongruously smooth.

"This is His Majesty's Royal Navy, Kent, not a damned church fête. We're not going to issue you a bloody invitation."

Sally jerked her chin into her collar to hide beneath the dark brim of her hat. She would have known that deep, laconic voice anywhere, even over the pounding din of the rain.

David St. Vincent Colyear.

But would he know her?

He had been eighteen years old and on the verge of taking his lieutenant's exam the last time she had seen him, the summer her brother Matthew had brought him home to Falmouth.

Col, they had called him. Six years ago, he had been long and lean, but by God, clad in the endless fall of his gray sea cloak, he was a leviathan now. A great oaken mast of a man looming up from the waist of the small boat.

A man grown. A man whose jaw looked as sharp as an axe blade and whose piercing eyes, the color of green chalcedony stone, were just as hard and impenetrable.

Sally pushed her voice deeper. "Aye, sir," she answered. "I'm Richard Kent."

"I know." Col's voice was low and dangerously soft—disconcerting in such a hard-looking man. "Now get in the bloody boat."

ABOUT THE AUTHOR

ELIZABETH ESSEX is a *USA Today* bestselling author of over twenty critically acclaimed historical romances, including the Reckless Brides and Highland Brides series.

Her books have been nominated for numerous awards, including the Gayle Wilson Award of Excellence, the Romantic Times Reviewers' Choice and Seal of Excellence Awards, and RWA's prestigious RITA Award. The Reckless Brides Series has also made Top-Ten lists from Romantic Times, The Romance Reviews and Affaire de Coeur Magazine, and every book in the series was awarded Desert Isle Keeper status at All About Romance. Her fifth book, A BREATH OF SCANDAL, was named Best Historical in the Reader's Crown 2013.

When not rereading Jane Austen, mucking about in her garden, walking her beloved dogs, Ghillie and Brogue, or simply messing about with boats, Elizabeth can be always be found with her laptop, making up stories about heroes and heroines who live far more exciting lives than she.

It wasn't always so. Long before she ever set pen to paper, Elizabeth graduated from Hollins College with a BA in Classics and Art History, and then earned her MA in Nautical Archaeology from Texas A&M University. While she loved the academic life of an underwater archaeologist, she has found her true calling writing lush, lyrical historical romance full of mystery, passion, daring and adventure.

Elizabeth lives in Texas with her husband, the Indispensable Mr. Essex, and her active and exuberant family in an old house filled to the brim with books.

Elizabeth loves to hear from readers, so please feel free to contact her at the following places:

ALSO BY ELIZABETH ESSEX

Reckless Brides

Almost a Scandal

A Breath of Scandal

After the Scandal

A Scandal to Remember

The Scandal Before Christmas (novella)

A Lady's Gift for Scandal (holiday novella)

The Difference One Duke Makes (novella)

She Walks in Scandal (novella in *A Midsummer Night's Romance* Anthology)

Highland Brides

Mad for Love (long novella)

Mad About the Marquess

A Fine Madness

Mad, Plaid and Dangerous to Marry

Mad Dogs and Englishwomen (Coming soon!)

Dartmouth Brides

The Pursuit of Pleasure

A Sense of Sin

The Danger of Desire

The Dartmouth Brides Boxed Set (with holiday novella "*Up on the Rooftops*")

The Kent Brothers Chronicles

Between the Devil & the Deep Blue Sea ~ and ~ The Devil's Own Luck

To keep up to date on new releases and events, sign up for Elizabeth's newsletter and get exclusive excerpts, contests, and more

http://www.elizabethessex.com

I also hope you'll take a few minutes out of your day to review this book – your honest opinion is much appreciated. Reviews help introduce readers to new authors they wouldn't otherwise meet.